I0723811

CONQUERED BY THE ALIEN WARRIOR

HOPE HART

Copyright © 2020 by Bingeable Books LLC

All rights reserved.

No part of this book may be reproduced in any form or by any electronic or mechanical means, including information storage and retrieval systems, without written permission from the author, except for the use of brief quotations in a book review.

The Arcav Alien Invasion Series

The Arcav King's Mate

The Arcav Commander's Human

The Arcav General's Woman

The Arcav Prince's Captive

A Very Arcav Christmas

The Arcav Captain's Queen

The Arcav Guard's Female

The Warriors of Agron Series

Taken by the Alien Warrior

Claimed by the Alien Warrior

Saved by the Alien Warrior

Seduced by the Alien Warrior

Protected by the Alien Warrior

Captured by the Alien Warrior

Rescued by the Alien Warrior

Enticed by the Alien Warrior

Conquered by the Alien Warrior

✿ Created with Vellum

CHAPTER ONE

S arissa

I creep along the castle halls, my footsteps light and exceedingly careful. I pause, breathe, and strain my ears.

No sign of movement. Still quiet. This castle is different in the dead of the night. Torches are lit at intervals along each corridor, their flames dancing as I pass. But the obsidian stone seems to suck up all that light, spitting it back out through the thin, gleaming silver veins cutting through the stone.

Beneath my dress, I'm wearing sturdy boots—broken in by hours of walking through the castle, the town nearby, and the marketplace. Those hours of walking and talking were worth it—giving me the contacts I need to sneak out of here and back to Rakiz's camp.

I take one more step, and the hair on the back of my neck stands up.

Suddenly, I'm back at the Farm after being recruited by the CIA, listening to my favorite instructor.

I freeze.

Your intuition exists for one reason and one reason only: to keep you alive. If you don't listen to it, you're ignoring a God-given gift.

I glance around. Still quiet. Deathly quiet. *Too* quiet.

Damn it.

I can't just stand here and wait. The attack against Vivian and Arix proved there are people in this castle that can't be trusted.

Sure, those traitors might be dead. But betrayal begins as a seed of bitterness and is watered by fury. Who knows who else might still have a bone to pick with the king—and his guests?

The corridors in this wing of the castle are like a rabbit warren, with little rhyme or reason. And yet from what I know about Arix, *everything* he does has a reason. My guess is these corridors are designed to confuse anyone who shouldn't necessarily be walking in this part of the castle.

I grind my teeth and walk faster. Two more intersections to go, and then I take a right. From there, I just need to jog down several flights of stairs in the servants' quarters, and I'm—

Slam.

Something comes out of the darkness, looming in my peripheral vision. I duck, automatically twisting, but it keeps coming. I blink, and my breath leaves me in a whoosh as I'm shoved against the stone wall, inches from a flickering torch.

The light from that torch spills over the commander's face, and I curse.

He smiles at me, but there's no amusement in that smile.

It simply amplifies the sharp planes of his face. The flames reflect back at me from his silver eyes, making him look like a demon who's come to drag me down to hell.

I squirm and writhe, but he's using his weight to hold me in place against the stone, his huge body like a slab of concrete against me.

Why do these Braxian men have to be so damn big?

I scowl up at him, and his smile widens. Trust him to gloat once he has me pinned.

"What do you want?" I hiss, careful to keep my voice quiet. The last thing I need is to wake up my cousin.

"Funny thing about human females," he says, ignoring my question. "No matter how quiet you think you are, your movements sound like thunder to my ears."

I scoff. He's lying. I'm great at being sneaky. He's definitely lying.

For sure lying.

Focus, Sarissa.

I bare my teeth at him. "And why would you care?"

"Because my king has charged me with making sure you don't get killed traveling back to *your* tribe without me."

I'd love to punch the smug look off his face, but it'd make too much noise. In one sentence—and with that tone—he's told me that a) both he and the king think I'd be killed if I traveled alone and b) I belong elsewhere and I'm sure as hell not welcome here.

It pisses me off.

"Well," I say sweetly, "it's not like Arix's little lapdog can think for himself, hmm?"

I don't think he knows what a lapdog is, but from his expression, the translator in his ear has given him a pretty good idea. All hints of amusement leave his face. And then he smiles again, and the gleam of his teeth in the dark makes me shiver.

It's probably not a good idea to piss off the Braxian commander, but I can't seem to help myself.

"I was told to make sure you don't leave alone, since you seem to have problems controlling your impulses. Our enemies have been spotted in many places between this castle and Rakiz's camp, and yet you believe you can go alone?"

He curls his lip at me, and I push against his chest, but he's not budging.

"You asshole. This castle is a shitshow. Your *enemies* almost killed the king *and* my cousin. Why would I trust any of your guards to go with me when they can't even be trusted not to attempt to murder their monarch?"

Korzyn's face goes blank, and I fight back a smile. Score. As commander of Arix's army and the man tasked with keeping the king alive, it must *burn* that so many people so close to the king ended up being dirty.

To be fair, Korzyn and Arix knew about most of the traitors, and they were playing a long game, drawing out anyone who would betray them so they could solve the problem in one swoop. Unfortunately, their schemes almost cost my cousin her life, and while *she* may have moved on, to me that's an unforgivable offense.

"We've solved that problem," Korzyn grits out.

I tilt my head. "Have you?" I smirk, just because I know it pisses him off. "Have you really?"

He's silent, and I almost cheer as his jaw tightens.

Unfortunately, I don't have time to hang around here and chat. My contact is waiting for me to get on his boat.

"Look, Korzyn, I don't want to argue with you. I need to get the control chip back to Alexis so she can start working on that ship and we can get off this planet. Unfortunately, I can't trust your guards not to be working with the Dokhalls, and if they get the chip, they'll either attempt to take the ship by force or destroy the chip out of spite."

His face looks like it's carved out of granite. "I don't care."

"Excuse me?"

"I don't care who you trust. I've made a deal with Arix, and that deal includes protecting your worthless life."

I roll my eyes. "Not if I can help it."

He grins, and this time he looks genuinely amused. I attempt to ignore what it does to me to see the hard lines of his face relax, those eyes lightening.

"You can't."

I frown, but suddenly I'm spinning in place, Korzyn's hands expertly twirling me until I'm facing the wall. I slam my head back, and he curses as I make contact with his face.

The scuffle is as quick as it is brutal. Within seconds, he has my hands caught in one of his, and he's deftly tying them behind my back.

I briefly consider screaming. If Vivian saw the commander manhandling me this way, she'd lose her shit. All it would take is one of Vivian's wide-eyed glances at Arix, and he'd order Korzyn to let me go.

Unfortunately, my pride doesn't allow it. I'm trained. I'd bet on myself against almost anyone in a fight. But I let myself be trapped against this wall and distracted, allowing Korzyn to get into the perfect position to pin me.

I fight to keep my voice steady. "I'll kill you for this."

Korzyn laughs, his voice low and muffled. I'm guessing he doesn't want to risk waking up my cousin and her sugar woogams either.

"You can try."

The words are wet, and despite myself, I grin.

"Nose a little sore, Korzyn?"

He leans forward and wipes his face against my cheek.

"Ew!"

His blood is warm, and I struggle instinctively, but it's too late. My wrists are bound.

Maybe I should just suck it up and scream. I'll collect the tattered remains of my ego later. I open my mouth only to choke as Korzyn takes the opportunity to shove a piece of material into my mouth, his hands quick as he ties it.

I slam my head back again, but he's not falling for that move twice. I'll have one hell of a bruise on the back of my head already, and he now knows I'll happily ring my own bell if I have to.

He throws me over his shoulder, ignoring my "oof" as his hard muscle digs into my belly. I shift in an attempt to knee him, but he clamps his arm around my legs. Then the bastard *slaps me on the ass* with a laugh and saunters down the hall.

My eye begins to twitch. I'm about to explode from either rage or sheer mortification.

Korzyn's quarters aren't far from mine. I should've known the commander would stay close. After all, he's made sure to follow me around since the moment I got here.

Thankfully, there are no guards outside Korzyn's door. Obviously, he's decided he doesn't need them. Or maybe he doesn't trust them. Either way, I'm saved from the humiliation that would occur if anyone else witnessed this nightmare.

Korzyn throws me onto his bed, and I wiggle until I'm on my back, staring up at him. He looks very pleased with himself, and there's something dark in his eyes as he scans me, lingering on the gag in my mouth.

"I think I prefer you like this," he says, and I glare at him so hard I'm surprised his head doesn't explode from my fury alone. "Now. Let's discuss what's going to happen next."

Korzyn

When I first learned how to grip a sword, I was young. So young I could barely lift it. My trainer had little patience and less empathy, and I was expected to swing that sword for hours each day.

My hands suffered. A particularly nasty blister formed on my palm beneath my thumb. Each day after training, I would bandage it, and it would begin the healing process only to pop open the next day. Eventually, it grew so large I had to hold my sword with my nondominant hand.

Years later, when I spoke to my trainer, I asked him why he wouldn't allow us to see the healers, who had balms that would have taken the pain from our blisters.

He laughed. "Would you have learned to swing your sword this skillfully with your left hand if your right did not pain you so?"

I glowered at him and stalked away, furious at his answer.

That blister plagued me, making it impossible to use my hand. Each time it got close to healing, I would be told to pick up my sword, bursting the protective layer and producing teeth-clenching pain. Eventually, the wound became infected, and my trainer had to relent and allow the healers to treat it.

The scar is now thick—a reminder that with every wound comes a healing. A hardening.

The female currently tied up on my bed reminds me of that blister.

Each time I see her, my protective layers burst and my jaw aches from clenching my teeth.

She is a stone in my shoe.

She glowers at me, and I allow myself a few moments to enjoy the satisfaction of seeing her tied up and helpless before me.

I'm not a spiteful male. I perform my duties, protect my king, and train with my men.

But I can't ignore the gratification I feel at seeing this vindictive female at my mercy.

It makes something tighten in my stomach, and I run my gaze over her, from her flushed face, to the pale skin above her dark-gray dress, to the worn boots on her feet.

She makes a strangled sound, beating those feet against my bed, and I laugh.

From the look on her face, she's planning my murder.

A spark of interest ignites before I can dampen it. It has been many years since I was concerned with anything other than protecting Arix from the numerous attempts on his life.

"Let me tell you what will happen now," I say, and Sarissa narrows her eyes at me. They're the strangest color —neither green nor blue but somehow both at once.

"You will sleep in here, as you can't be trusted not to attempt to sneak out of this castle and I need to rest before our journey."

Her eyes flash at me, and I can't help but grin. I haven't felt this light for days.

"That's correct. I'm going with you. We leave at dawn, so I suggest you get some sleep."

She gives me a look so scathing that if I were a lesser male, I would wither under it.

"If you agree not to scream, I will remove your gag. Not that anyone would come for you, but it's time for me to rest."

She nods, and I lean forward. Her legs tremble, her feet twitching as if she is fighting the impulse to kick me in the head, and I almost smile. This female is not stupid. If she knocks me out, she will be stuck in this room, gagged and bound, until I awake. And then I will be furious.

"Look," she says when I untie the gag, "why don't you just tell Arix you went to get me but I'd already escaped?"

Her tone is cajoling, as if she's attempting to reason with me, and I almost laugh.

Instead, I slowly shake my head. "No. I have made a deal with Arix. If I take you back to Rakiz's camp, he'll give me something I very much want."

Her eyes sharpen with interest. "And what do you want?"

"That doesn't concern you."

Her lips thin, and her ire makes my shoulders lighten with amusement.

"I can't sleep like this," she says.

"Too bad."

"Korzyn. My hands will be damaged if I sleep with them like this. This rope is cutting off my circulation."

I'm not an idiot. She's hoping I will free her and she will somehow escape. However, Vivian will be upset if her cousin is damaged, and when Vivian is upset, Arix is enraged.

"Roll onto your side."

She thinks about it for a moment but finally complies. Her tiny feet shift, likely as she again debates whether to kick me, and I feel the strangest urge to...laugh.

She huffs out a breath as she turns over, and I take

another long piece of material, tying it around her right wrist.

"Make a fist."

She does, letting out a snort when I loosen it slightly.

"Have a lot of experience tying up women, baby?" The human endearment is heavy with sarcasm, and I grit my teeth.

"If there was ever a female who deserved to be tied to a male's bed, it's you."

She lets out a strangled noise, and I push her onto her front, enjoying her muffled growl. I tie the other end of her new tether to my bedpost before removing the cloth tying her hands together. Since I'm a merciful male, I allow her to have one hand free so she can sleep easier.

I withdraw as she flips onto her back. She glances up at where the material is attached to my bed and again rolls her eyes.

I study her face. She seems entirely too calm.

"Where are your weapons?" I ask.

"Hmm?"

From the lift of her eyebrow, she's attempting to pretend indifference. That means the female probably has at least one knife hidden somewhere. A knife she would likely use to free herself before castrating me in retaliation.

I smile. "You know, the guards are still talking about the way your cousin killed Bevix. A poisoned dagger. Brutal yet elegant. Not only did she get the poison in his bloodstream, but Arix said the way she threw that knife at his throat was a thing of beauty."

Pride flashes in Sarissa's eyes. "Vivian has always had exceptionally good aim."

My smile widens. "You know what I found most interesting about that?"

"I'm sure you're going to tell me."

"No one knew she had a knife. Otherwise, our enemies would have taken it from her."

From the rage burning in the hellion's eyes, she knows exactly what's going to happen next. She lets out a shriek, and when I push up her dress, this time she does kick out.

I freeze. Her thighs are pale, toned, and ridiculously smooth. But from her knees down, long scars trail across her shins, onto the tops of her feet.

"What happened here?" The long white scars wind around her legs like ropes. A small part of me pities her. The pain must have been excruciating.

"None of your business."

Her other hand is free, and she aims it at my head, growling when I catch it.

"Let me go, perv."

I smile at the sheath strapped to her thigh. "Is this knife dipped in poison?"

"You'll find out when you least expect it," she vows, and I laugh.

She stares at me, likely unused to hearing me make such a sound. Truthfully, I'm also unused to making it.

"Where are your other weapons?"

She clamps her mouth shut, and I sigh. I check her boots next, encountering not one but two small daggers. I run my hands up her arms, finding another knife. I frown at the long piece of metal wrapped around her upper arm.

"Jewelry," she tells me, and I sigh, removing the metal band. While even I can admit this female is beautiful, there's no doubt she doesn't spend much time on her appearance. Her lady's maid was imprisoned after working with our enemies, and the castle gossiped relentlessly about how

Sarissa refused to take another maid, choosing instead to get ready alone each day.

The only jewelry I have ever seen her wear are the blue stones in her ears. If she wants me to believe the strange piece of metal in my hand is jewelry, she'll be disappointed, because it most definitely is not.

Her eyes darken with frustration. But she stays silent.

"Is this all?"

She nods, and I sigh.

"I'm tired. Don't make me search the rest of you."

She pulls at her hand, still trapped in my fist, and I let it go with a warning look. Her hand disappears down her dress, between her breasts, and she pulls out a thin knife.

My mouth drops open. The woman is a walking armory.

She smirks at me. "I want these all back in the morning."

I study her. She's waiting for me to agree, one eyebrow raised.

"Where is the last weapon?"

She growls, gesturing at the pile next to me on the bed. "Are you kidding me? You just took it."

I reach into the pocket of her dress, pulling out a pile of papers. One of them is a map of this part of Agron, and I study it with interest. "You've been busy."

She ignores that, and I place the papers next to her weapons.

I survey every inch of her, going as far as to make her roll onto her stomach as I run my fingers along her spine. She shivers, and I ignore what that does to my body.

"No knife here?"

"I have a bung shoulder. I can't reach for it quickly."

I almost concede, but while her face is a blank mask, she can't hide the hint of triumph in her eyes as I begin gathering her weapons.

I lean forward and pull the ornate pin from her hair. Her golden locks tumble down around her face, and this time, she's truly furious.

I study the hairpin, unsheathing it and whistling as I poke the sharp end. "I haven't seen these before."

"I had it made for me," she grits out.

I meet her eyes. "I wouldn't have known, but you rarely wear ornaments in your hair."

I don't know why I feel the need to explain, but she's silent as I move her weapons away. I'd think her cowed if not for the resentment that burns in her eyes.

"You will rue the fucking day you decided to come after me. Do you hear me?"

I smile at that, placing her weapons on the table by my window.

Sarissa keeps talking. "I bet taking my weapons and tying me up makes you feel like a man."

I scowl at that. This female has an uncanny ability to annoy me, which she uses ruthlessly. And I usually can't help but retaliate.

I pick up another piece of material, ignoring her gasp of outrage as I take her free hand. She bucks, kicking out, and I narrowly miss her foot as she aims at my balls.

Vicious female.

I tie her other hand to my bed. Turns out I'm not a merciful male after all.

"You're right," I say. "It does make me feel like a man."

She stays sullenly silent, and I sigh, pulling one of my blankets from the bed. I leave the rest for the hellion and walk toward the long sofa in front of my fire. She casts the flames a wary look, and I frown at her.

"Go to sleep."

CHAPTER TWO

S arissa

I hate the commander.

I've always hated him, of course. But before this, I hated him the way you'd hate a bad boss, or a colleague who took credit for your work.

It was a distant kind of hate. One I could put aside when I wasn't near him so I could focus on other things.

Now my hatred for him is all-encompassing. My hands shake, twitching with the urge to wrap them around his wide neck.

I wouldn't kill him, of course. That would be more than a little awkward for my cousin. But I'd love to choke him out, tie him up, and leave him cursing my name.

The thought fills me with warmth, and I allow visions of my revenge to float through my head. Korzyn doesn't know it now, but he has fucked up big time.

Revenge is a dish best served with a punch in the face.

I glower as he rolls over again, the crackling of the fire the only other sound in the room. Truthfully, we don't need a fire, but earlier, he ran his eyes indolently over my body and added another log. The implication being, of course, that I'm a scrawny, weak human who needs to be kept warm.

I haven't slept a wink. The hours crawled by as I waited for the commander to go to sleep so I could figure out a way to get free, collect my weapons, and still hopefully make my boat. All the plans I've made, ruined by the commander. Typical.

I'm not dumb. I have every mile of my journey mapped out. I've got contacts on both this side and the other side of the water, all waiting for me. Tonight, once I crossed the water, I was supposed to walk east for about a mile until I came to the tiny town of Hexir, where my friend Weva's sister, Teriez, lives. I planned to spend the rest of the night there before leaving at first light and walking back west until I reached the forest.

From there, I would have made my way to Rakiz's camp, staying with friends and contacts along the way. It shouldn't have taken more than a few days on foot, and I have backup plans for my backup plans.

I scowl. The commander hasn't seemed to sleep any more than I have. At one point, I began tugging on one of my hands, certain I could feel weakness where it was connected to the bedpost. Korzyn sat up and let out a low growl, vowing that if I didn't stop, he'd come and sleep next to me.

The room is lighter now, and I'm sure the sun is rising. By now, I should be across the water and on my way to Rakiz's camp.

I blow out a frustrated breath. I'll just have to adjust my plans. The commander will definitely cramp my style. But if leaving with him is what I have to do to get the chip to Alexis, then that's what I'll do.

I may fantasize about burying the commander alive, but I can still see the bigger picture.

And that picture includes revenge against the Grivath for daring to think they could fuck with human women without repercussions.

Korzyn has obviously given up on sleep as well because he rolls to his feet, cutting me a glare as he stalks toward his curtains and throws them open.

A knock sounds at the door.

"Come in," I call, my voice carrying over Korzyn's "not now."

The servant blanches as she walks in, her mouth dropping open as she takes me in, her gaze lingering over my hands still tied to the bed. Korzyn closes his eyes for one long moment, and I barely suppress a victorious grin.

"I know, right? The commander is into some dirty, dirrrrty stuff. Spread the word."

Korzyn growls out a curse, and the servant begins backing away.

"Don't leave," I call out. "I need breakfast."

My toes curl, and I almost explode with laughter as the servant enters with her tray, placing it on a table near the window. She stares at the pile of weapons sitting on that same table.

"Oh, that," I say. "The commander enjoys knife play in bed. It makes him feel like an alpha."

"Sarissa," Korzyn snaps, his voice like ice, and the servant blushes, hurrying away. Once she's gone, I can't hold it any longer. I burst out laughing.

"Okay," I say, wishing I could wipe the tears off my face. "That was hilarious. Now untie me."

"Naughty females don't get untied."

I scowl at him. "My bladder says they do, unless you want me to let loose allll over your bed."

He raises one eyebrow at that but prowls over to me, eyeing me as if I'm a poisonous snake.

He swipes one of my blades as he passes the table, and it looks tiny in his huge hand. When he leans down, I hold my breath so I don't have to breathe in the male scent of him. He slashes the material holding me, and I slowly pull my wrist away from the bed, scowling at him as I rub my skin. He raises one eyebrow in a way that suggests I'm being a drama queen.

Dickhead.

He slices the other piece of material and retreats back to the food, picking up a piece of fruit. I roll off the bed and stalk toward the bathroom attached to Korzyn's room. I can feel his eyes on me, but I carefully ignore him as I open the door.

I immediately scan the room for weapons, but I'm out of luck. I take care of business, wishing I could lounge in Korzyn's huge tub positioned next to a window overlooking the gardens. In the distance, the river winds through the castle grounds, cutting through the town and toward the marketplace.

I wash my hands, scowling into the mirror. Since Korzyn took my pin away, my hair is tangled, the blonde strands falling around my face. It makes me look younger, and much more innocent than I've ever been.

There's a reason I don't like to leave my hair down. When I catch a glimpse of myself in a mirror, I see Claire, running wild through our childhood home.

I turn away, open the door, and immediately meet Korzyn's gaze. "I need my weapons back."

He snorts, and I simply raise one eyebrow.

"Are we or are we not traveling together? I need to be armed."

"I will protect you."

"Yeah, that's not going to work for me."

Standoff. Finally, he sighs and gestures toward my weapons. I don't have a heart attack from the shock, but it's a close call.

I narrow my eyes at him.

"We will have an escort to the dock," he says. "In case you're having any thoughts about taking your weapons and running away."

I frown, but the sound of the door opening brings full realization.

"Sarissa Quinn Davis! I got your note," my cousin says from behind me. Korzyn's face stays blank, but amusement flickers in his eyes at my groan. "You were going to sneak out of here without letting me know?"

I whirl. "Korzyn trailing after me is *your* fault?"

Arix steps behind my cousin, giving me a warning look. I roll my eyes.

She scowls at me. "It sure is. I knew you'd run, and I expressed my concern to Arix."

"You know I could've easily gotten back to Rakiz's camp alone," I say. "That big dumb commander is nothing but a liability who'll draw attention to us both."

Korzyn makes a strangled sound behind me, and Vivian lifts her hand, covering her mouth as her eyes laugh at me.

"I know you could. I also know you've made more than enough contacts to go alone. But I'd worry the whole time. Please, can't you just take him with you?"

Vivian holds her hands up in front of her as if begging, and I open my mouth to refuse, but Arix's eyes harden. I sigh. The big guy wouldn't look so stubborn if he didn't truly think my cousin would be upset with me going alone.

For a moment, resentment burns. I had a plan, and without Vivian's interference, I would've been well on my way back to camp by now.

At first, we assumed Dragix would stop by the castle. After all, he was bringing a few of Vivian's friends here every day after she was almost killed. When he didn't show up to collect the chip, we sent a message to Nevada. According to her, the dragon has been out hunting for days.

I stayed here for Vivian's coronation. I even twiddled my thumbs for a few more days, waiting to hear back about Dragix. Finally, the control chip began consuming my every thought.

Each moment the control chip is in my possession is a moment Alexis and Kate aren't installing it in our ship.

"Fine," I bite out, sighing at Vivian's hurt look. I soften my tone. "I'll let the commander crash my party."

"Great," she says. Her gaze searches my face, and she attempts a smile. "We'll walk you to the dock."

I glance over my shoulder to where Korzyn is lounging by the window, suspiciously silent. He's doing his usual blank face, but the corner of his lip twitches—the only sign he's appreciating his victory.

Whatever Arix promised him must be a doozy.

Korzyn

The hellion is quiet as we walk toward the dock. Before we left, she collected her weapons, excusing herself to the bathroom, where she obviously slid them all back into place.

When she returned, her hair was in a sleek bun, held up with her lethal hairpin, and she looked calm and composed.

I ignored the urge to pull out that pin, if only to enjoy the way her eyes would flash at me when she bared her tiny teeth.

She's irritated with her cousin. And from the glances Vivian keeps sending toward her, she's likely picking up on that annoyance. Arix grinds his teeth, frowning at me, and I shrug in return.

I'm holding up my end of the bargain.

The bargain he forced me to make.

His words repeat in my head each time I think about turning down this trip with Sarissa.

"Viv loves her cousin. She needs her to be safe to remain happy. If she finds that Sarissa is traveling alone, she will worry. She may even cry." Arix looks murderous at the thought. *"I don't care how either of you feel about each other. You will both fall in line. You will take her to that camp, and you will not let her get one scratch I can't explain to my queen."*

I raise one eyebrow. I do many things for Arix. I've risked my life for him since I was little more than a young boy. But spending so long with the barbed female is out of the question.

"And why would I subject myself to that atrocity?"

Arix smiles, and it is a very satisfied one. "Because I will tell you which female you kissed at my mate's coronation."

I tense. "What do you know of it?"

He shrugs. "You spoke about it for days, revealing all the details. It was only a matter of time before I was able to narrow down my suspects."

I consider that. Vivian's coronation was on Seva—the night once a year when thousands of shooting stars take over the night sky. After dinner, almost everyone wandered outside, standing in groups or finding quiet spots to sit and watch the incredible sight.

I'd been flirting with a noblewoman all night. She was from Mazark's territory, with dark hair and darker eyes, and when I sat down alone in the darkness, she sat next to me, wrapped in a cloak to keep her warm from the chill of the night.

She no longer talked or giggled. Instead, she looked up at the sky and sighed as if her heart was breaking.

I was surprised when she cuddled close, unused to females being so forward. But her scent drew me in, somehow so different and yet familiar at the same time.

Within moments, I cupped her face, taking her mouth the way I wanted to take her body. She yielded to me, letting out the tiniest moan that I captured with my lips.

Voices intruded, and she jumped to her feet, backing away. Later, I described every inch of her to Arix, who claimed not to know who she was.

"You found her?"

He shrugs, and I glower at him.

"I've put my body between yours and any who would harm you for my entire life, and you won't give me a simple name?"

Arix's jaw tightens. "One day, you will find a female for whom you would sacrifice anything to see her smile, and you will understand. For now, I offer you a trade. Make sure both Sarissa and that chip arrive at Rakiz's camp in one piece. It will only take a few days of your time, and I will give you the name."

So here I am, climbing into a boat with Sarissa, who looks just as displeased as I am. She's right about one thing, however—choosing to take guards with us would be a mistake. Particularly since they likely know she's traveling back with the chip.

That reminds me. "You should give me the chip."

She wrinkles her nose at me. "Not on your life."

I rub my temple in an attempt to ward off the headache

that is beginning to throb there. Sarissa blows a kiss at her cousin, who grins at her.

"Promise you'll be careful," Vivian calls.

"Of course. I'll see you soon."

I shift, attempting to ignore the way the boat rolls as the captain takes us further from the dock. Like most Braxians, I hate the water.

I glance back at Sarissa. "I will keep the chip safe."

She snorts. "Uh-huh. Not gonna happen. Nice try though."

I shrug. I'm not sure where Sarissa could be hiding the chip, but if it's anything like her weapons, it's likely well hidden. Either way, I have a greater chance of standing up to torture than she does.

I open my mouth, and she narrows her eyes at me.

"No."

"Fine."

I shrug again, but I vow to find out where she's hiding the chip. Arix's deal included delivering both the female and the chip, and I'm not going to risk my potential mate because of this female's stubbornness.

CHAPTER THREE

S arissa

I sigh as I stare up at the mishua. The trip across the Colossal Water only took a few hours. Now the hard part begins.

I hate riding mishua.

First of all, the beasts only allow males to ride them. Or at least, steer them. I could sit on a mishua's back and encourage it to move for hours, and it wouldn't go anywhere until the moment a Braxian male tied it to his own mishua.

It's infuriating.

Apparently, Nevada managed to convince a mishua to let her ride it when she went looking for the other human women—shortly after they crash-landed here. But it took her days to persuade the mishua before it would tolerate her on its back, and even then, Rakiz was convinced it would have killed her by the time he found her.

This is why I was planning to bypass the mishua altogether.

Sure, a mishua would get me to Rakiz's camp faster, but I figured as a female traveling alone, it was smarter for me to go on foot—so I could easily hide when necessary. Plus, I can go days without sleep, and I had my contacts lined up along the way in case I needed shelter.

Unfortunately, Korzyn disagrees.

"A mishua will get us there much faster."

"Only Braxians ride mishua. It's a good way to announce to our enemies we're here and traveling alone."

"Speed is of the greatest importance."

"Yeah. I'm sure you've got a busy social life to get back to."

He narrows his eyes at me. I narrow mine back.

"This is what we're doing," he says finally, and I grind my teeth.

"You make it really easy to hate you."

He flashes his teeth at me and gestures for me to get on the mishua. Behind him, one of Rakiz's warriors is looking on in amusement. Dexar and Rakiz quickly realized they would need to keep mishua here for when their people wanted to travel across the water, and they've surrounded the mishua pen with guards.

I smile at the warrior, who has incredible dark-green eyes. "I can leave the commander here to watch the mishua. You wanna come with me instead?" I ask him, and he grins at me. He runs his eyes over my body, and Korzyn goes very still next to me.

"Get. On. The. Mishua."

I sigh. Better to pick my battles. "If we get targeted because we're on this stupid mishua, I'm telling Arix it was all your idea."

The mishua tenses as I mount her, one of her red eyes focused on me. Viv says they're smart and can understand more than we think, so I've likely just made an enemy of my lizard horse as well.

Awesome.

Korzyn mounts behind me, and my mood turns darker at the feel of his ridiculously hard body pressed against mine.

"Move back. You're in my space," I snipe, and he ignores me, reaching around me and directing the mishua out of the paddock.

"Her name is Heli," Rakiz's warrior says, stepping back.

"Awesome." I wave goodbye to him, ignoring Korzyn's low growl.

"Why are you so pissy? You didn't have to come."

"Yes, I did."

"You gonna tell me what Arix offered you in exchange?"

"Why would I?"

Now I'm even more curious. But I clamp my mouth shut. "Fine."

"I will tell you in exchange for an answer to one of my questions."

Hmm. I consider this as the mishua plods further from the pen and toward the forest. Soon we'll need to be quiet, careful not to draw any attention to ourselves.

Despite myself, I'm desperate to know what could have made the commander agree to this trip when he so clearly wants to be elsewhere.

The king could technically order him to go with me. But from what I've observed, the two are close friends. If Arix is giving the commander something he wants, then I want to know exactly what it is.

Knowledge is power, after all.

"Fine," I say. "You tell me first."

He moves slightly in the weird mishua-shaped saddle, and the leather creaks beneath us.

"On the night of Arix and Vivian's mating, after Vivian was coronated…"

"Yes?"

"The crowd left the ballroom to see the shooting stars."

"I remember." It was Seva, and Arix insisted we all go outside. I shrugged, looking for solitude. I didn't find it, but I became entranced with the shooting stars anyway.

"I met a female that night."

I suddenly feel…uncomfortable. "Uh-huh. And?"

"She was a noblewoman from Mazark's tribe. We talked…briefly—"

I smirk. "You mean you flirted."

"Yes. I had thought that was all it was. Truthfully, I wasn't looking for anything more."

Korzyn is being surprisingly open and honest. I glance over my shoulder, but his gaze is on the horizon, his face thoughtful. He's basically thinking aloud, and it's as if I'm not even here.

I stay silent, waiting for him to spill the rest of the details.

"I wanted to watch the stars alone. So I found a dark corner of the gardens. It was close to the tree the children like to climb."

Oh shit.

"The noblewoman sat next to me, and we looked up at the stars. Within moments, we were kissing."

Uh-oh.

"I don't know her name."

I shuffle uncomfortably on the mishua, ignoring the way the beast narrows her eye at me.

The noble Korzyn thought he kissed?

Yeah, it was me.

I didn't know it at the time, of course. I'd been flirting with one of Arix's guards all night, and like most people, I was pretty hammered after all the noptri. Vivian insisted I take a cloak, and I wandered out into the garden in an attempt to make the world stop spinning.

I plunked myself down next to the guard, a guy named Heros, who was staring up at the shooting stars as if they'd tell him the secrets of the universe. I glanced up too, somehow still shocked at just how different the stars were on Agron compared to Earth.

It made me feel small, and it reminded me Earth was very, very far away.

When he leaned closer, I decided to numb the pain in a way that noptri hadn't quite managed to do.

The kiss was the kind of kiss you force yourself to lock away because if you ever let it free again, you'll lose hours examining it from every angle.

It started off the way all kisses do, my lips brushing his. And then Heros took control, sliding his arm behind me and pulling me close as he explored my mouth. I lost all track of time until the peaceful night was broken as a group of people walked close by, their laughter bringing me back down to earth.

I pulled away, my head spinning as I got to my feet. Heros turned toward the sound, the light of a shooting star hitting his face at just the right moment, and I suddenly felt stone-cold sober.

It wasn't Heros at all.

I'd just made out with the commander.

I hurried to bed, swearing to never think of it again and figuring Korzyn would do the same.

Instead, he made a deal with Arix.

I chew my lip. *Could* Arix know it was me?

I was hungover the next morning. Was that knowing look Arix gave me at breakfast because he knew I'd swiped a bottle of his best noptri or because he knew I'd kissed his commander?

I reasoned I had no need to tell Korzyn. I figured he'd move on—likely that same night. I never imagined he would care.

I take a deep breath and slowly let it out. He can never know.

Korzyn has fallen silent, and I clear my throat awkwardly. I have no idea what he just said.

"So you kissed a mystery woman and now you want to know who it is?"

"Yes."

"Why do you care so much?"

He shrugs. "I've answered your question. Now you will answer mine."

"Fine."

"Where are you hiding the control chip?"

***

Korzyn

Sarissa goes still in front of me. "Sneaky commander," she says, her voice cold.

"We have an agreement."

"I'll tell you if you swear you will never take it from me."

"You agreed to tell me anyway," I say, and her body becomes even tenser, making the mishua throw her head in annoyance.

I sigh. "I swear I will not take it from you."

"It's inside my earring."

I raise an eyebrow at that, leaning forward to examine the small blue stone in her right ear.

"How?"

"These earrings aren't exactly high-quality, but I was wearing them when I was taken, so I've kept them in my ears. The blue jewel part is fake—it's too big to be real, especially on my budget. So I pried it out and filed it down until the control chip could fit between the jewel and the prongs."

I have to admit, the female is exceptionally intelligent. I never would have thought to check the small stones in her ears.

"That is a good hiding place."

"Thanks." The word is slightly sarcastic, and I'm sure she is annoyed I used my question to discover her hiding place.

Her annoyance pleases me, and I sit back in the saddle, content.

We ride in silence, making our way toward Rakiz's camp. At one point, we slide off the mishua to stretch our legs, and I reach into one of my saddlebags for rations, my stomach grumbling.

"Food?"

Sarissa shakes her head, and I frown.

"Are you still upset because I know where your precious chip is?"

"No."

I take a bite of dried meat, following it with a swig of water as I study her face. She's staring into the distance, her expression dark.

I shrug. "Let's go."

Sarissa turns toward the mishua and then freezes, her eyes wild. I open my mouth, but then I hear them.

Voices.

Sarissa is scanning the area, and I can practically see her creating and discarding plans. She glances at the mishua and then gives me a withering look, and I know she's still convinced we shouldn't have used the beast.

I give her a look of my own, positioning the mishua behind a group of trees, hidden from the voices to the left of us.

"Silence," I quietly warn the mishua, who ignores me.

Sarissa is crouching behind a bush, and I crouch behind her, my hand on my sword. The voices are coming closer, and Sarissa slides one of her daggers out of the sheath hidden in her boot.

The voices belong to Dokhalls, who come close enough that I can see their purple skin through the bush. Sarissa is practically vibrating with tension in front of me, and I place my hand on her shoulder. She jumps, giving me a dirty look, but she lets out a long breath, some of the stiffness leaving her body.

The Dokhalls pass, and Sarissa slowly gets to her feet. Within moments, she's stalking after them. While I mocked her for making too much noise in the castle, I have to admit she's almost silent as she prowls after the Dokhalls.

I follow, careful not to disturb the forest around me.

While we've been traveling by mishua, we've mostly avoided the main paths throughout the forest. This was lucky because the Dokhalls have set up their own rustic camp here, building structures out of tree branches hidden just off the path.

"They're trying to cut off Arix," Sarissa breathes, peering

around the trunk of the tree she's hiding behind. "Anyone who comes through this path won't be expecting an attack."

I nod, grinding my teeth. We will have to be even more careful, likely taking days longer to get to Rakiz's camp. But the sooner I get to the camp, the sooner I can find the dragon and convince him to get a message to Arix, warning him not to send anyone after us.

"Let's go," Sarissa murmurs, and we make our way back to the mishua. We will have to find an alternate path, and quickly.

I blink, suddenly dizzy. Sarissa scowls at me as I stumble, and we both freeze as a branch cracks beneath my foot.

We barely breathe, but I have to bend over, my hands on my knees as bile rises and I fight to stay on my feet.

"What are you doing?" Sarissa hisses.

"Dizzy," I mumble.

She takes my elbow. "What the hell, Korzyn?"

I focus on making it back to the mishua as the world swims sickly around me. What could have happened?

"Bush. Poisonous?"

Sarissa shakes her head. "No. I was closer to it and I'm fine."

"Poison," I insist, and both Sarissas in front of me frown in disbelief. Realization crosses both their faces just as a third Sarissa joins them.

"The food," they say, dancing in front of my eyes. "I haven't eaten anything, but you have. Someone poisoned our food."

I push away the betrayal that instinctively rises. I have been protecting Arix from such attacks for so long that it never occurred to me I would be targeted.

There's no reason to kill me now that the king's enemies have been found. No reason except for revenge.

Someone in the kitchen was working with Bevix.

"Need to warn Arix."

"You *need* to get on the mishua," Sarissa snaps. Four other Sarissas also nod their heads in agreement.

I blink, and my eyes stay shut. Something cracks across my face, and I manage to pry my eyes open.

There's only one Sarissa now, and she's pale, her eyes flashing.

"Blue," I mumble. "They're blue now. Pretty blue."

"Fuck," Sarissa mutters. She wedges herself beneath my shoulder, throwing my arm around her neck. "Just walk. I'll figure this shit out."

I'm so dizzy I'm having trouble seeing the world around me. Distantly, I know this is a bad sign. "Death by dried meat," I mumble. "Humiliating."

Sarissa snorts. "I told you not to come with me. Okay, the mishua is right here. All you have to do is help me get you into the saddle."

I nod, but my chin falls forward and my eyes slide closed.

CRACK.

"You enjoyed that," I say, managing to open my eyes to slits. Distantly, I can feel my cheek burning with the force of her slap.

"Of course I did. Get your shit together."

I feel my lips curl. For some reason, I occasionally find her abrasiveness charming. "Vicious female."

"Get on the mishua."

I can vaguely see the beast dancing in front of my eyes. Sarissa inhales sharply, likely realizing just how bad our situation is.

"Okay," she says. She takes my hand, directing it where it needs to go. Then she kneels, and I shift my weight to my right foot as she raises my left one and places it in her cupped hands.

"Use me as a step stool."

The female will only be able to handle my weight for a short moment. I collect every last drop of my remaining energy and shake my head in an attempt to clear it.

"You got this," Sarissa says, and I chuckle.

"Are you...encouraging...me?"

"Sadly, your well-being is now directly tied to mine. On three."

She counts down, and I push up. The female is stronger than she looks, offering a good amount of resistance as she pushes against my foot, helping to boost me into the saddle.

"I'm sorry," I murmur, and the world goes black.

CHAPTER FOUR

S arissa

"Korzyn?"

Unconscious. Fuck.

We're in deep shit right now. I glance toward the path the Dokhalls took. We need to stay even further from the main path, which is going to add even more time to our trip.

I glance up at Korzyn. He's worryingly pale.

"I knew you were a liability," I mutter.

He doesn't reply, and I take the mishua's head, looking deep in her eyes. "You either walk where I lead you with him on your back or I leave you behind for the Dokhalls. Do you understand?"

The mishua snorts, but I'm not messing around. Either she behaves or I'll figure out another plan. If I have to drag Korzyn through the forest myself, I'll fucking do it.

Of course, I could always leave him.

I sigh. It's one thing if I kill him myself. It's another if I leave him to die while he's vulnerable. There's no honor in that.

Plus, Arix might kill me.

I grind my teeth. If I'd been allowed to go alone, this never would've happened.

Well it did happen, Sarissa. So what are you going to do about it?

I pull out my map. I could head back toward the mishua pen. There are other guards there who may be able to help. Making my way to Hexir is out of the question now. According to the information I bargained for, there are a few caves to choose from, although those came with warnings to be careful not to end up in a wild karja's lair.

There's a cave not far from here. It won't be comfortable, but if we can hunker down there, I can figure out what to do next.

Okay. The commander isn't looking good at all. His lips have a bit of a blue tint. Is his breathing labored?

Another instructor's voice sounds in my head. *"It's not the situation that will kill you. Panic will take you out first. Don't let your own response be the determining factor in your death."*

Zoey taught me a little about plants before I left. I walked with her in the forest a few times, soaking up as much information as I could. If I can find a particular plant, it may help draw the poison out of the commander. But first, I need to get him somewhere safe.

The cave it is.

I tug on the leather strap around Heli's nose. For a moment, she digs in her heels, and I bare my teeth at her.

"I will kick your ass."

It's an empty threat. If she lowers her head any further, she'll probably gouge me with those vicious-looking horns.

Korzyn groans on her back, and she jolts into motion, almost stepping on my toes.

I give the Dokhalls a wide berth, heading deeper into the forest. The mishua takes soft, quiet steps, but I'm still tense, my largest knife clutched in my hand as I scan my surroundings for threats. I stop often, listening for any more Dokhalls. But each time I glance at Korzyn's face, I move faster.

I'm dripping with sweat by the time we arrive at the rocky mountain on the edge of the forest. The cave entrance is small, but I ignore my claustrophobia and force myself to go inside, checking for animals.

The cave is much larger inside than it looked from the outside. Since no wild animals are leaping at me, ready to tear my face off, I duck my head and inch inside the cave, my eyes slowly adjusting to the dim light.

Water drips down the walls toward the back of the cave, but the front is dry and—if I can build a fire—should allow us to stay relatively warm.

From the small pile of furs on one side of the cave, I'd say it's been used as a hunting cave by one or more of the Braxian tribes near here—likely why there are no animals to be seen.

My shoulders slump as I blow out a breath, and I walk back to where the mishua is being surprisingly patient as she waits.

"Korzyn?"

I keep my voice low, but I shake the commander. He groans, and I poke him until he manages to crack open one eye.

I gasp.

The white surrounding his silver eyes has turned bright red. He lifts his head slightly, and I curse.

His nose is bleeding.

It's just a little blood, but from his condition, it's evident that whatever poison he was given is fast acting.

I've lost too many people. I refuse to lose any more. Even the commander who drives me insane.

"Get off the mishua," I order.

"Leave me."

"I can't until you're in the cave."

His movements are painstakingly slow, but I manage to get him off the mishua, where he collapses to the ground. Anxiety makes my voice sharp.

"Get up."

"I thought there would be peace in death."

"You thought wrong. Let's go. I don't have all day."

I urge him to his feet, although I'm almost carrying him as we move into the cave.

"You know, this is the second time I'm saving your dumb ass."

He lets out a weak laugh at the reminder of the way I saved his life in the marketplace. I brought him the head of the Zinta that stabbed him, and my cousin almost threw up at the sight. Next, I'd love to get my hands on whoever decided to poison our food.

But revenge plans are for later.

"I saved you too, vicious female. You were wandering alone and bleeding through the forest when Arix and Vivian were attacked." He lets out a low growl at the thought.

"That's different. I'd already taken care of the asshole who thought he could hold me hostage, and I was making my way back to the castle. Duck," I say as we get to the cave entrance.

He lowers his head, falling to his knees as soon as we're

in the cave. I'd prefer for him to be further inside, but he's once again unconscious.

If I don't find that plant, he's dead.

I leave the mishua tied to a tree. I'll need to find water for her later. Actually, since we can't trust our own rations, I'll need to find water for all of us.

I stalk through the forest. After Zoey taught me about ortar—a plant used as an antiseptic—I pointed to a plant sitting by the sun in her poison kradi. "What's that?" I asked, and Zoey smiled.

"That's the only hope for anyone who happens to ingest one of my poisons."

Which means it's the only hope for Korzyn as well.

I crouch, examining a group of plants pressed up against the trunk of a tree. I'm looking for a plant with leaves so dark they're almost black. The underside of the leaves are distinctive—with light- and dark-green stripes.

I can do this. I just have to go to the empty place inside myself where there's nothing except logic.

That empty place is why it's likely I seemed cold and unfeeling when everyone else was falling apart on that ship. I wasn't unaffected by our circumstances. I was just already attempting to figure out how the fuck we were going to survive. I didn't have time to fall apart.

And you don't have time now, so get moving.

My hands are shaking as I lean down and check under the leaves of a plant that's similar to the one I need. Zoey told me the name in Braxian, and it's almost unpronounceable, but I've mentally dubbed it the zebra plant.

An animal rustles nearby, and I take out my knife again. I'm a city girl through and through, and the sounds of the forest put me on edge. There are all kinds of critters out here, many of them with sharp teeth, scary claws, and/or deadly poison.

I bend again, using my knife to push up the leaf of a plant so I can check beneath it. Zoey taught me not to touch anything I don't recognize. God, I wish she were here now.

I wish *anyone* were here now. If the commander dies...

Head. In. The. Game.

The forest floor is beginning to rise in an incline, and I peer through some of the trees at a large hill. If I can climb up the hill, I can try to get the lay of the land. Hopefully, I can use it to figure out where the Dokhalls are.

But first, the plant.

Zoey said it tends to grow near the base of the white trees, so I begin focusing my attention there. I don't know how long it's been when I finally find what I'm looking for, but triumph floods my body.

I dig up the plant, brushing off the roots. I need to boil the roots in water and then make Korzyn drink the water, or he's toast.

Water. I can hear the bubbling of a stream close by, but I'll need to find something to boil the water in first.

I clutch the zebra plant in my hand. The poison struck so fast...

I walk as quickly—and as quietly—as I can through the forest and back toward the cave.

The sun is already going down, and I'm panting when I get back. I give the mishua a pat on the head as I find a small pot for cooking in one of Korzyn's saddlebags. I spin around and head back toward the area where I heard the water before crouching on the side of the stream and filling the pot.

I carry it back to the cave and almost drop it as I stare down the commander.

At some point, he stripped off his shirt, displaying smooth muscle and golden, tan skin. I can't help but examine the scales across his chest and shoulders. The blue-green marks him as a descendent of dragons, reminding me how different we are.

And yet my hands itch to stroke those scales.

Whoa. Obviously, stress and exhaustion are getting the best of me.

I force my gaze back up to his pale face, letting out a rough curse. He looks...dead.

I lean my face close to his.

"Still breathing," he mutters. "Or were you hoping to kiss me before I died?"

I jerk away, my face coloring. "I was trying to see if it was worth wasting my time saving your useless life," I snap.

His eyes are still closed, but the hint of a smile plays around his mouth. He may look worse than he ever has, but at least he's regained consciousness.

"Rest now 'cause soon you'll be drinking this water like your life depends on it."

Because it does.

He ignores that, falling back to sleep, but his breath is shallow and uneven. It hitches occasionally, and I find myself listening for him to take the next breath, and the next.

I force myself to back away and get to work making a fire. It takes a few trips to find the right kind of wood, and I mentally high-five myself for buying the expensive fire-starting coils I found in the marketplace.

Within about half an hour, I have the water boiling, and I put some clean water aside for me to drink later. Then I drop the roots of the zebra plant into the rest of the water to let it steep. The roots are a dark red, and they stain the water until it looks like blood.

Gross.

I check on the commander again. He's shivering, but his forehead is damp with sweat.

Fever.

I can't wait any longer.

I take the water off the fire, dipping a cup into it. It feels like it takes forever for it to cool down enough to drink, but as soon as it's no longer scalding, I shove one of the commander's saddlebags beneath his head so he can sit up.

"Korzyn?"

No reply.

Roaring fills my ears.

"You don't get to check out after I've gone to so much effort to keep you alive," I snap. "Open your damn eyes."

I cajole. I whine. I attempt to pour some of the water down his throat, but he starts choking.

"Come on, Korzyn. Please."

He cracks open his eyes, and they're so red they match the color of the water.

"Never...thought I'd hear...you say...please. Must...be...dying."

"Yeah, yeah. You're not dying. Now hurry up and drink this."

I make him drink most of the water. He attempts to stop, and I threaten to pour it over his head.

He glowers at me, but his color is slightly better when we finish. Is his breathing more even as he closes his eyes?

I'm exhausted. I feed the mishua, drink some of the clean water I put aside, and curl up next to the commander, watching his chest rise and fall.

CHAPTER FIVE

S arissa

The aliens jeer at us, poking their sticks through the bars. We fight over space as we all attempt to flatten ourselves against the wall, but we know how this ends.

We've been on this ship for days, and it appears our captors are bored because they've decided we're their entertainment.

"Dance, human, dance!"

Blaire bares her teeth. "Fuck you."

This makes one of the purple aliens incensed. He slams his palm print on the screen by the door as if ready to come into the cage and drag her out.

I step to the front of the group. If he comes in this cage, I'll rip out his throat with my bare hands. From the expression on some of the other women's faces, they're thinking the exact same thing as me.

One of the other aliens pulls him away from the palm screen.

The first alien lashes out. He reaches his stick between the bars, catching Kelly in the shoulder. The expression on his face is savage as she screams, falling to the ground with a smell like burning hair. The other aliens pull him away, but the damage has been done. I slump to my knees, my brain going blank as I stare at the beautiful young life that has just been snuffed out for no reason at all.

The aliens are fighting amongst themselves, with one of them screaming and waving his hands at the bastard who just killed Kelly. A door opens, and all the other aliens go silent as the one who is clearly the leader walks down the steps. He takes one look at Kelly lying dead in our cage, and he gestures at the alien next to the one who killed her. I'm so numb I can't even feel happy when the alien who killed Kelly is killed in front of us as well. I turn my back on all of them as women erupt into sobs around me.

The aliens leave us alone with Kelly's body. One of the women next to me looks like she must only be sixteen or seventeen. She curls up into a ball on the floor, rocking herself as she whispers something under her breath over and over again. I lean closer.

"We're going to die, we're going to die, we're going to die."

My heart breaks for her. I was seventeen once. And while life wasn't good, it certainly wasn't this hell.

"Hey there, what's your name?"

She glances at me, still repeating her words on a loop. "Winter," she says. "We're all going to die."

I survey the cage, the pale faces, the trauma clear in everyone's eyes. And I get to my feet.

"Listen up," I say. "What just happened to Kelly should never have happened. She deserved to live. We all deserve to live. We need to play this smart. They want us to dance? We'll do a fucking jig if that's what it takes. We are going to get out of here alive, and when we do, we are going to make the Grivath pay for everything they've done to us. And we're not going to stop there.

We're going after these purple bastards. Humans are no longer going to be sitting ducks. They may have taken us unaware, but I promise you, if we work together, this will be just another shitty memory we bury under our beds with all the others."

"And how, exactly, are we going to do that?" a voice pipes up.

"We need to make plans. So far, all we've done is be victims. And that's okay while we're stuck in the stupid cage. But it won't always be like this. These bastards want to sell us, which means that one day, we're walking out of this cage. And we need to be ready. Who's with me?"

I jolt awake, certain I can still smell the unwashed bodies of the other women around me. But it's another scent that fills my nostrils, a masculine scent. I sit up, examining the commander's face. He's still so pale he looks like a corpse, but when I place the back of my hand against his forehead, it seems as if his fever isn't quite so high. He's no longer shivering anyway.

"Korzyn," I say, but he doesn't respond. Well, at least he's still alive.

The light in the cave is dim, and I roll to my feet, my entire body aching. I wander out of the cave and check on the mishua, who eyes me, obviously displeased with her situation. I refill her water and stumble off into the bushes as my bladder howls at me. I need to get to the top of that hill. The Dokhalls were close yesterday. We didn't make it far from where they were hiding near the main path.

I don't want to leave Korzyn for long, but I should probably find some more of the zebra plant anyway. I keep an eye out for it, feeling the muscles in my legs stretch as I make my way back toward the hill. The sun is rising over the forest, and I'm surrounded by the scent of greenery. Okay, maybe Zoey was on to something when she insisted the forest was peaceful. As long as I don't worry about exactly what else could be out here with me, I can admit the silence is good for thinking.

The hill is steep enough that I have to lean forward, concentrating on where I put my feet. The ground is crumbly and dry, and I curse as a prickly bush slices across my ankle above my boot. The sun is high in the sky by the time I get to the top, and I'm out of breath, no longer used to being this active after so long lounging around the castle. In the distance, the water beckons, and Rakiz's camp lies behind me—northwest of here. I survey the forest around me, scanning it for threats, and my mouth goes dry.

To the northeast, smoke curls above the trees. I've learned to listen to my intuition, and it's screaming at me that the smoke doesn't belong to Dragix. Of course, I won't know for sure until I can get closer. And I can't do that until I'm sure the commander won't die on me.

I pull my map out of my pocket and compare it to what I can see in front of me. I crowdsourced most of what's on my map from people who know the topography and geography of this planet much better than I do. It means I can pinpoint approximately where I am in comparison to everything else.

I gingerly make my way back down the hill, careful not to slip. The last thing we need is for me to break an arm or leg. I find another zebra plant and take it back to Korzyn, who's still asleep. He's not unconscious though, and I managed to bully him awake and pour more of the gross plant water into him. He wrinkles his nose, which I take as a good sign.

He immediately falls back to sleep, and my stomach rumbles. This is not good. We can't trust any of our food.

I've gone without food before. In fact, the human body is remarkably resilient when it comes to going without food. My body will go into ketosis around forty-eight hours after my last meal. That means it'll start living off my fat stores. Unfortunately, my time on the ship with the Dokhalls wasn't good to me. I'm still putting on some of the weight I lost in captivity.

I rake my eyes over Korzyn's body. Something tells me it takes a lot of calories to feed that huge body. At the very least, I should be able to find some fruit, maybe a handful of nuts. I leave the commander sleeping and make my way toward the smoke.

Korzyn

I blink open my eyes, groaning as light seems to stab into my brain. I slam my eyes shut, then slowly crack them open, my head pounding at the effort.

I stare up at the ceiling above me, noting the rocks. I'm in some kind of...cave?

It all floods back. Losing consciousness on the mishua. Stumbling into the cave. The certainty I was dying. Sarissa, forcing me to drink bitter, slightly musty water.

She saved my life.

I grit my teeth.

And I doubt the hellion will let me forget it.

I attempt to sit up, but I can't even raise my head without the world spinning around me. I growl. I'm weaker than a babe.

Where is Sarissa now? Has she...left me?

No. The female may be vicious, even diabolical at times, but she is loyal to her core. Her words as she bullied me onto the mishua run through my mind.

"Sadly, your well-being is now directly tied to mine."

So where is she?

Uneasiness curls through my gut. I fall back into a light sleep, but I'm restless, continually waking and listening for her footsteps.

Finally, I sense her near, and I open my eyes.

Hers are a cool, clear green today, and the dark circles beneath them make it evident she had little sleep.

"Well," she says. "You're still alive."

"Where were you?" My voice is hoarse, and I curse how weak it sounds.

"Scouting the area. We have a problem. First, you should probably have more plant water."

I scowl at that, and her lip trembles before she firms it. She's obviously amused by my disgust.

"It's one of the only plants on Agron that's used as an antidote to many poisons. I have no idea what they used in our food, but it's all we have."

It burns to admit it, but... "You saved my life. Thank you."

Her eyes widen slightly at that. "Well." She clears her throat, her gaze darting awkwardly. Then she leans over and picks up a cup, bringing it to my mouth. I reach for it myself, but my hand is shaking too much to hold it.

"Just let me do it," she says, and I clench my teeth but allow it.

Fear winds through me. What if I don't recover? I would prefer death to this weakness and lethargy.

"Your eyes are looking better."

I must look confused because Sarissa smiles slightly. "The whites of your eyes were completely red, and you were bleeding from your nose. I thought you were a goner when you passed out that last time."

The knowledge of how close I came to death doesn't sit

well with me. If I am to die, it should be in battle with a sword in my hand or while protecting my king.

"Whoever did this will pay."

Sarissa nods. "We need to get a message back to Arix. And we also need to get out of here. But...there's an issue." She chews on her lower lip, and I force my gaze away from her mouth.

"What issue?"

Her eyes turn stark, and I realize she's no longer cool and collected. She's afraid. Protective instincts I thought were long dead begin to rise, and I reach for her hand. She freezes, and I move to pull my own hand away, but she turns it over, pressing her fingers to the pulse of my wrist.

"Dokhalls. They've set up some kind of camp to the northeast. We always knew they were around somewhere, but it explains why Rakiz's guards haven't located them yet —it's further from Rakiz's camp than we thought."

"You went without me?"

She pulls her hand away. "Oh, I'm sorry, should I have dragged your limp body with me?"

Don't strangle the hellion.

She snorts at me as if reading my mind and moves away before returning with a handful of berries, which she offers to me.

I'm not hungry, but I force myself to eat. I must regain some strength if we are to get out of this cave.

"Anyway," she says. "I need to get closer so we can figure out what they're doing and just how many of them there are."

I begin to nod but freeze as the thought of her going alone makes my gut clench. "No."

"Excuse me?"

"It's not safe."

"Let me be very clear. I'm not asking you. I'm telling you. We can't do shit until we can get you back on your feet, but if we stay in this cave, we're sitting ducks. We need to gather intelligence."

"I don't like it."

"I can't fully express to you how little I care."

I stare at her. "What exactly did you do on your planet?"

"I told you. I worked for an organization—"

I snort. "It's just you and me now, hellion. And I may not make it. Why not be honest?"

Her eyes sharpen at that, but she nods. "Fine. I was a spy."

I knew it. The way she bartered for information in the castle, the contacts she made, the people she became close with...

She grins. "Are you okay? Your eye is twitching. Are you about to have a stroke?"

"I knew you couldn't be trusted."

She rolls her eyes again. "I haven't used anything I learned against Arix, and I have no plans to. After all, he's on our side."

I grind my teeth, and she shrugs at my silence.

"Anyway, you stay here and rest up while I go check it out."

"We need to talk about this."

"Someone has to do the legwork while you get your strength back, princess."

I don't know whether to strangle her or kiss her.

I blink at that thought, and I must look horrified because Sarissa frowns. Is that...concern in her eyes?

"What's wrong? Are you in pain?"

She reaches for more of her disgusting water, and I wave it away.

The hellion is going to go without me, regardless of my thoughts on the matter. I would be wise to remember she can likely take care of herself.

"If they catch you, death would be a mercy."

She grins. "They won't catch me."

CHAPTER SIX

S arissa

Despite my tough talk, my hands are clammy as I creep closer to where I saw the smoke. There's no smoke at all today, but I've already memorized where I need to go.

Korzyn's right about one thing: if they catch me, I'll soon be wishing for death.

Behind me, a bird suddenly shrieks, and I jolt, cursing my jumpiness. As soon as I get close enough to the Dokhalls that I can hear voices, I shimmy up a tree. It's hard work—the bark is smooth beneath my fingers, and by the time I manage to find a secure branch to sit in, I'm panting.

I peer between the leaves, wishing I had binoculars. From here, I can see small structures, like kradis only made out of tree branches. They look like they'd blow away at the first storm, and I snort. The Dokhalls obviously aren't used to living rough.

I need to get closer.

I slide back down the tree, slowly make my way toward their camp. I stop every few feet, huddling behind trees and bushes, my ears straining to pick up any sound that doesn't belong.

Eventually, I find a large tree, similar to an oak on Earth. Finally, something is going right. I haul myself onto the lowest branch and then climb steadily until I'm high enough to see over the Dokhalls' camp but low enough to still be hidden by the leaves and branches.

There are more Dokhalls than I could have imagined. The structures I saw were just the start—likely a guard post. There must be several hundred Dokhalls swarming around the area, many of them carrying the long sticks they used to murder Kelly.

Without the ship, those sticks gradually begin to lose power. In our last battle with the Dokhalls, most of their weapons only had enough power to stun us.

That doesn't mean they're not dangerous though. All it takes is a few precious seconds of inattention to lose your life.

Sweat drips into my eyes as I cling to my branch, unable to pull my attention away from the camp. The reason Dragix hasn't been able to find it? It's hidden—not just beneath the canopy of trees but beneath an actual canopy, which the Dokhalls have created from some kind of net.

I survey the canopy above me. How the hell did they get it up so high?

It's covered in dirt, leaves, and unless my nose is wrong, shit. The Zintas have obviously taught the Dokhalls every-thing they know about hiding from the dragon.

Speaking of the Zintas...

On my left, close to one of the larger makeshift huts, a

group of Zintas are sitting with a few Dokhalls. From the deference the Zintas seem to be paying to the Dokhalls, I'm guessing they might be the leaders of this little gang.

I squint, but I'm too far away to see if one of them is the leader from our ship. I owe him some pain before he dies.

A Voildi walks through the tent, a scroll in his hand, which he gives to one of the Dokhalls. It appears that all the Braxians' enemies have decided to work together.

Lucky us.

God, I wish Dragix were here right now. He'd solve all our problems.

I tilt my head as I examine the canopy above me before surveying the entire camp and the trees surrounding it.

Maybe I don't need Dragix after all.

My hatred for the Dokhalls is all-encompassing. It consumes almost all my thoughts. With their blockage of the main road leading from the water, plus what is clearly a gathering of their troops here, it's clear they're planning to march toward the ship.

Our ship.

I clench my hand tighter around the hilt of my knife. I need to do whatever I can to delay that until we can get our own armies together. Arix promised to help, but we need to ensure he can actually get to Rakiz's camp, and it's crucial that he knows to expect the Dokhalls on that main path.

My mind is racing as I climb down the tree, and I'm consumed with possible ways to wreak havoc. I drop to the ground, about to turn, when something jabs me in the back.

I freeze.

"Human," an amused voice says. "You made a mistake coming here."

I raise my hands above my head, slowly turning.

A Dokhall grins at me. I don't recognize him from the ship, but from the expression on his face, he recognizes me.

"Drop your weapon."

I drop my knife, and his grin widens.

He jerks his head toward the camp. "Now walk."

I let my shoulders slump. I can't muster up a tear, but I sniffle anyway. From the triumph in the Dokhall's eyes, he believes I'm terrified.

Idiot.

I take a step, hugging my arms as if attempting to make myself look smaller. I pull one of my daggers from its sheath and spin, throwing it through the air.

I'm not expecting to hit him. Unlike my cousin, I'm not exactly a great shot. But the Dokhall still has to dodge the dagger, giving me a few precious seconds to lean down and swipe my larger, longer knife. It's about the length of my forearm, and while it can't compare to the Dokhall's stunner, at least it gives me a chance.

I need to get rid of this guy before more of his purple friends join him and I'm really screwed.

He bares his teeth and advances on me, his stick held like a spear.

I sigh. "You know the problem with you guys? You're so reliant on your special sticks that you don't know how to fight. Tell me, does that one even have any charge left? Or are you just expecting to hit me over the head with it?"

"Kill you, human."

I raise an eyebrow. "Well, that escalated quickly."

He won't kill me. Not so close to the camp when he'd be rewarded for taking me alive. I step away from the tree, giving myself more room to maneuver, and he strikes.

I dodge, and his weapon hits the tree, the sizzle it makes telling me it's not completely useless.

I force myself to laugh.

"Nice work, dipshit. Do you perform that poorly with your other stick too?" I wink at him, and he roars, charging me.

Fuck. Someone definitely would have heard that.

I drop to the ground and roll away as his weapon hits the ground next to my head. Shit, that was close. I roll closer toward him and slide my blade along one of his bare feet.

He howls, and I laugh.

"Hurt?" I get back to my feet, and he comes at me, weapon raised. He's faster than I thought, but I whirl, striking at his side. He blocks it with his weapon, pushing my knife aside and slamming the point of his stick into my shoulder.

Zap!

I go flying, my teeth clenched. Turns out his weapon has just enough juice to be dangerous. I roll straight back up to my feet, blinking furiously in an attempt to clear my vision. I can hear voices coming toward us, and from the grin on the Dokhall's face, so can he.

The muscles in his legs tense before he moves, and I lunge toward him, dancing across the forest as we strike and parry. My shoulder burns, but I clench my teeth. He has a better weapon, and he's stronger. But I'm faster.

He's getting tired. If he were smart, he'd be jabbing his weapon at me. Whatever power it uses comes from the tip, and he's more likely to incapacitate me that way. But he's getting angry and sloppy, wielding his weapon like a sword.

My heartbeat begins to pound in my ears as the voices get closer.

Screw this.

He lifts his weapon, teeth bared as he attempts to slam it into my head. I wait until the last possible second and pivot, tripping him off-balance and slamming him into the ground.

He rolls, but it's too late. I bury my knife in his chest, and he opens his mouth to scream. Panic rises, and I slit his throat, turning his scream into a choked moan.

I need to get out of here.

I lean down and swipe his weapon before sprinting away from the camp and back toward the cave. My shoulder aches, but I force myself to pump my arms faster, jumping over fallen trees and rocks.

I can't lead them anywhere near Korzyn. I backtrack, heading toward the water, and then hunker down behind a bush, waiting for my breath to steady as I plan out my next move.

***

Korzyn

I find myself unable to sleep while the hellion is away from the cave.

It's incredibly inconvenient.

At this point, it's crucial I recover, and yet each time I close my eyes, I see Sarissa, her lips trembling as the Dokhalls drag her into a cage. Sometimes, she's screaming, begging for help.

All while I'm lying here, useless.

She's an untrustworthy liability. So why does this terror make me desperate to go after her?

I managed to get up today, practically crawling toward the cave entrance and finding a spot to relieve my bladder behind a tree nearby.

Unfortunately, while I made it back to the cave, I passed

out in front of it, and I've been lying here ever since—unable to sleep but also unable to drag myself inside.

I grit my teeth and again attempt to move back into the cave. If Sarissa finds me here, I'll never hear the end of—

"What the hell are you doing out here?"

I turn my head, finding her out of breath, a scowl on her face. She has a shallow scratch along her forehead, and she's covered in dirt, but she's furiously alive.

I ignore the relief that washes through me.

"I wanted some fresh air."

She takes one look at me, lying in the dirt near the mishua, and a smile plays around her lips. I frown. It's more difficult to ignore her beauty when she isn't scowling at me.

I manage to sit up, leaning against a rock. "What happened?

"It's not good." She raises her hand, waving one of the Dokhalls' weapons, and bile burns at the back of my throat at the sight. "I was stupid and got too close." Her lips twist, and she sighs. "I had to kill one of them and haul ass back here. They'll be looking for whoever did it."

"You're lucky you weren't killed."

She sniffs. "Luck had nothing to do with it. I should've been paying more attention though. Unfortunately, I was preoccupied by the shitshow in front of me."

"What are you talking about?"

"The Dokhalls are gathering an army. And they're doing it under cover of the forest. They've set up a huge net above the trees, and it's covered in dirt and poop so they can hide their scents from Dragix. There were hundreds of them, and from what I saw, they were getting ready to march."

I close my eyes. "They'll send scouts ahead."

Sarissa nods. "Yes. And they'll likely be moving fast. They'll spread them out in all directions, and unless they're stupid, they'll leave more groups in key places, blocking off anyone who thinks to help."

I once again curse my weakness. "We need to leave."

She rolls her eyes. "Sure, get on your feet, and let's go."

I scowl at her sarcasm, and she scowls back.

"I have the beginning of a plan."

CHAPTER SEVEN

S arissa

To say Korzyn is unimpressed with my plan is putting it lightly.

We argued most of the night before I forced more of the disgusting water down him and we both fell asleep. Thankfully, the cave is warm enough if we huddle together, but this morning, the air was colder than it has been so far, and I found myself fantasizing about crawling on top of the commander.

To steal his heat, of course.

"Look," I say. "We have to do something. We're running out of nuts and berries, and they're just not cutting it. We need meat, and while I'm good at many, *many* things, hunting and trapping and skinning animals are not any of those things."

Korzyn tilts his head, raising one eyebrow, and I shove a few berries in my mouth.

Sometimes, Korzyn seems to be doing better. He made it outside the cave again last night. Other times—like right now—it appears as if he's still on the path to death.

His blinks are slow, and it seems to cost him energy just to open his eyes again.

"You are desperate to get that chip to your friends. It's clouding your thoughts."

"It's driving me toward my goal," I argue, and he snorts.

"Your obsession will get you killed."

"It's a good thing I don't need your approval."

"Explain to me why this must happen so quickly."

"You mean other than the army of Dokhalls who are definitely sending out scouts to find us?"

He nods, sighing at whatever he sees on my face. "Please."

I turn away, gathering my weapons.

"Imagine the worst thing that could happen to you," I say. "Imagine it comes out of nowhere. And imagine it doesn't only happen to you, but it also happens to a group of other women who are just as scared as you. Some of them are younger, some of them older, but all of them need to believe in something."

The commander clears his throat. "So you gave them something to believe in."

I nod. "I made promises I shouldn't have. I promised we'd get through that trip on the ship, that we'd survive, and that we'd get revenge. I promised no one would ever hurt us again and that we would thrive. I promised anything and everything under the sun. I threw out hope like I was throwing candy at a group of children at a birthday party. I said whatever it took. Now I have to deliver."

"That doesn't explain why your urgency is so great."

"One of the other women, Clara, accused me of shirking

my responsibilities when I traveled with Vivian," I murmur. "She said I was a leader who was happy to risk her life but not her heart and it wasn't fair for me to leave when the other women needed my emotional support." I sigh. "She was right. I crumbled under the weight of their neediness. I couldn't face having to look at those women every day, knowing I was responsible for their lives. They put their trust in me, and when I get this chip back to them, they'll know it was warranted."

I stare at the cave entrance. Sometimes, I wake up, still expecting to be on that ship.

Why did I give those women what was likely false hope? Why was it so important for me to convince them we were getting off that ship? That we wouldn't die? Or worse, be used as sex slaves?

Maybe my need to save them comes from the fact I couldn't save the only person who counted. Who knows? All *I* know is I keep my promises. I'll do whatever it takes to make sure those women get their lives back.

Korzyn is quiet, and I glance over my shoulder. His eyes are closed, but I know he's not asleep.

"Your plan is flimsy," he says. "You're allowing your emotions and overinflated sense of responsibility to drive your actions."

That strikes just a little too close to home, and I grind my teeth. The commander is making it very, very easy for me to go through with the first step of my plan.

"I need you to take the chip," I say.

"Excuse me?"

I shrug. "If I get taken, they'll search me, and they might find it. You're slowly recovering, and eventually, you'll be able to sit on the mishua. If I don't make it, you need to get the chip back to Alexis."

He opens his eyes, his nostrils flaring. "There is no need because you're not leaving."

I roll my eyes. Trust him to make this more difficult than necessary.

"We'll have to agree to disagree. Either way, I'm starving. I'm going to go see if I can forage us some more food."

"Swear to me you're not going to their camp."

"I'm not."

"Give me your word."

"I give you my word I'm just going to pick a few plants and scrape together whatever food I can find. I'll be back soon."

He studies my face and then finally nods, his eyes sliding closed.

He's not going to enjoy what happens when I get back.

By now, I know the best spot to find berries, but I'm also in luck, and I find a tree bursting with a type of fruit called a dorza—a cross between an apple and a mandarin. I eat a few right there, wishing I had some form of protein, and then gather a few more, stopping to pick one juicy maradoza berry.

I need to be careful. This is how Zoey killed the Dokhalls who mistakenly kidnapped her and Nevada. But it's most commonly used by the healers for knocking out patients before surgery or ensuring they recover from painful injuries.

I don't want the commander dead; I just want him to take a nice nap.

The fact is he can't follow me. After staggering outside last night, he was so weak that he fell into a deep sleep for hours. But it's clear he's not resting properly when I'm away from the cave.

And we both need him to recover.

I'll err on the side of caution. I'd rather the berry not work than to work too well. An enraged commander who wakes up alone is better than one who doesn't wake up at all.

I break the berry in half and then squeeze a tiny amount of juice from the berry into the commander's zebra-plant water when I return. His eyes are still closed, but I know he's awake because a muscle is jumping in his jaw.

"Drink this."

He's strong enough to hold the cup for himself this time, and he gulps it down.

While he drinks, I feed the mishua the last of her food and make sure she has clean water. When I return, Korzyn's eyes are heavy-lidded, liquid silver as he stares at me.

"What?"

"You have a scratch on your face."

I shrug, fingering my forehead. "It's fine."

"You should take care of it."

"I'll find an ortar plant later."

I move closer to the commander, suddenly drawn like a moth to a flame. "You know, you never told me why you were so certain I couldn't be trusted. You followed me around like a stalker the entire time I was at the castle, but you basically gave Vivian a free pass. Why?"

He shrugs, the movement languid, and his head rolls. "You do your best to avoid attracting attention unless it benefits you in some way to cause a distraction. You lie easily and charm without thought, and it was clear you were gathering information about us."

I nod. "That's fair. But if I'm so untrustworthy, why do you care if I attack the camp?"

He opens his mouth and seems to change his mind

about whatever he was going to say. "I only get the name of my female if you're returned to Rakiz alive."

I ignore the way his words make something in my chest twist. I'm going to enjoy what happens next.

"All the things you named are some of my best qualities, and that's why my plan will work," I tell him. "Luckily, I don't need trust, approval, or anything else from you."

My throat feels tight, and I turn away, gathering the things I need as his eyes close.

"Dizzy," he mutters. "What did you do?"

"Just a little something to help you sleep."

He lets out a low growl, but I lean over, tying his wrists together before he can realize what I'm doing, then I wrap the rope around the tree root sticking out of the cave floor.

In his current condition, Korzyn is going nowhere.

His eyes fly open as he tugs at the rope.

I smile. "Payback is a bitch. Don't worry, I won't gag you."

"Kill you."

"Toughen up, buttercup. You did the same to me. I'm just looking out for you. You're safe here, so go to sleep, recover, and we'll chat when you wake up."

If he regains his strength, the rope won't hold him for long. But I don't need it to. I've carefully thought out each step of my plan. Including the next one.

His eyes are slits, and I feel like his prey as I slide my earring out of my ear. I lean forward and poke it through his shirt, fastening it next to his neck.

"If I don't come back, tell the other women I'm sorry. Tell Vivian...tell her I went out with a knife in my hand. And tell them to have good lives. Lives they'll be proud of."

"Don't you dare," he growls, tugging on the rope. I study his face, and I don't know what comes over me because I lean closer and brush my lips against his, wishing for...something.

He goes silent as I pull away, but his eyes are blazing. "If you leave me here, I will hunt you," he tells me, his voice very quiet and all the scarier for the control he's using. "I will make you wish you had never been born."

I smile at that, but my heart cracks as I get to my feet. "You'll have to get in line."

CHAPTER EIGHT

S arissa

I was born during one of the worst storms of my parents' generation. My mother said it was a sign of things to come. She said *I* was a storm and just like the day of my birth, my life would be turbulent and angry. She once told me I would never know peace.

She was a hateful woman, consumed with herself. My father was just as bad, too self-involved to even make sure our smoke detectors were working properly.

At the time, I sneered at my mother, pretending I didn't believe her. But deep down I knew she was right.

When I was abducted, it was barely a surprise.

That's the thing about storms. They ruin, they devastate, but eventually, they always die—leaving peace behind. Until they appear elsewhere.

I may never know peace. That's okay. But if I'm a storm, I'm going to ravage this galaxy until I find the

Grivath. And then I'll make them pay for what they did to us.

I stalk away from the cave, and as soon as I'm far enough from Korzyn that I can no longer hear his roars of outrage, I pull my map out of my pocket and study it. I'm not egotistical enough to think I can pull this off alone. And if the commander were able to walk in a straight line without falling on his face, I'd happily take his help.

But what am I supposed to do—let us be sitting ducks until he's better?

I don't think so.

Still, I feel oddly...lonely as I make my way through the forest, giving the Dokhalls' camp a wide berth. My journey is agonizingly slow as I'm careful not to draw attention to myself.

I need to cross a river to get to Hexir, and I can feel the hair on the back of my neck stand up as I walk across the skinny bridge. I raise my eyebrow at the blackened ground on the other side of the river. There's no vegetation for about twenty feet between the edge of the river and the forest.

Dragix has obviously been in the neighborhood, and from the look of the place, he wasn't in a good mood.

I walk through the ash and to the blackened trees at the outskirts of the forest, gritting my teeth against the urge to break into a run now that I'm out in the open. As soon as I'm back in the shade of the trees, my shoulders slump, and I have to lean against a charred tree trunk—my legs trembling as I come down from the adrenaline.

I make it to Hexir by early afternoon—judging by how high the sun is in the emerald sky. It's certainly not a large town—more a collection of tashivs than anything else. I hide behind a tree for a while so I can ensure no Dokhalls have taken up residence here.

I turn my map over, reading my notes. Apparently, Teriez's house is just outside of the town, backing onto the forest. I'll be able to spot it thanks to the flowers in the window.

I sigh as I stare at the three houses in front of me. All of them have flowers in their windows.

I wander through the town until I find a few houses that are backing onto the forest. Nothing else for it. I march up to the first one and knock on the door.

An old woman opens the door, a dagger in her hand, fear on her face.

"I'm not here to hurt you," I blurt out. "I'm looking for Teriez."

"Two tashivs down," she says and slams the door in my face.

I can feel eyes on me, and I fight back the urge to pull my own knife as I walk toward the tashiv. I knock on the door, and a shirtless man opens it, a sword in his hand. He has Braxian features, blue skin, and horns, and I must've been on this planet for too long because it's a surprisingly attractive combination.

"Yes?"

I eye the sword. "I'm looking for Teriez."

"Who are you?"

He's not rude, more...curious.

"Sarissa. Her sister, Weva, sent me."

He grins, revealing straight white teeth. "I'm their brother, Urox." His grin widens at my raised eyebrows, and he gestures to his blue chest. "Half, obviously."

Urox is so easygoing that I can't help but smile back. "Is she home?"

He opens the door wider. "Come in."

Teriez is sitting in front of a fire, boiling some water. She wrinkles her nose as I walk in, and I blush. Yes, it's been a few days since I bathed. And yes, I'm well aware I must stink.

"You must be Sarissa," she says. "My sister told me you'd be coming."

"Yes. I'd hoped to travel alone, but Arix's commander came with me. He's sick, and the Dokhalls are gathering an army."

Urox leans against the doorway, his eyes shining with interest as I explain everything that's happened.

"So let me ensure I understand you correctly," he says. "You dragged the poisoned commander onto a mishua, got him into a cave, saved his life, spied on the Dokhalls, killed one of them, drugged the commander, and snuck through the forest to get to us."

I think about it. "Yep."

He throws back his head and roars with laughter. "You're my kind of female."

Teriez smiles at that. "Ignore my brother," she advises me. "How can we help?"

"All I really need is a distraction."

Teriez runs her eyes over my ripped dress, her gaze lingering on the cut on my forehead. "You need more than that. Sit down, and I'll make you some food. Then you can wash."

"I don't have time. The commander—"

"The commander is likely in a deep sleep if you gave him maradoza berries," Urox says. "Teriez is right. You're not going to be able to hit the Dokhalls until after the sun sets anyway. I'm guessing you have a plan?"

I smile at him. This is the kind of support I need in my life.

"I sure do."

Korzyn

I stare up at my father. Why must I leave our camp? I have a home here. My mother has another babe in her belly, and I play with my friends each day.

"It is time," he says.

"Father..."

*"Remember what I said, Korzyn. Your purpose is to protect the king. That is your **only** purpose. Do you understand?"*

My mother's lips are bloodless, her eyes filled with tears as she hugs me goodbye. She immediately turns away, as if she can no longer look at me.

I have seen fourteen summers. I'm one of the strongest of my friends and the fastest with my sword. But had I known I'd be sent to train as a guard for the new king, I would never have spent so long improving my sword skills.

I crack open my eyes as I attempt to reach out for my mother, but my hand is tied. A cave. My mother isn't here. I'm in the cave. And there's something I must do...

I struggle, but it's no use, and I'm once again pulled under.

"Too slow," my trainer tells me. "You are to be the last defense between the king and those who would kill him. What happens if you are too slow?"

I grit my teeth, blood running down my face from the cut along my cheekbone.

"He dies."

"He dies, and the entire kingdom of Heriast knows it was because his guard was too slow."

"Korzyn?"

I turn at Arix's voice, and my trainer bows. "Your Majesty," I murmur.

Arix waves his hand. "You know I hate formalities. Are you ready for the hunt?"

I gesture at my bloodied clothes. "I will clean up and meet you in your quarters."

He grins at me, and I blink. For so long I have resented this young king, who was responsible for the loss of my home—even if he was not aware of it. But...he is honorable. Kind. He has the potential to be a great ruler, if I can keep him alive long enough for him to consolidate his power.

I blink open my eyes, the cave dancing in front of me.

The little witch drugged me. I pull at the ropes around my wrists, not missing the irony. I tied her to my bed, so she returned the favor. If she had not left to throw her life away, I would almost be amused.

I groan, but my eyes are too heavy, sliding closed once more. I grit my teeth. Not again.

I'm in the marketplace, the crowd's shocked whispers surrounding me after the sudden attack. The attack I was too distracted to see coming.

Sarissa stands in front of me, her face white as she stares at the wound in my chest. She drops to her knees.

"Serves you right for stalking me," she mutters. "Oh God, there's so much blood. You need a healer."

"Cava berries," I manage to get out. "Right pocket."

She pulls them out, stuffing them in my mouth. I can feel my blood draining onto the ground around me. When my pocket is empty, she takes my sword and gets to her feet, eyeing the crowd around us.

Is she...guarding me?

The world turns dark, and then I'm lying in the healers' quar-

ters, insisting that Arix find the little hellion who chased after the Zinta that stabbed me.

She appears, the Zinta's head clutched in her hand, and I can't help but laugh as her cousin gags.

"Vicious female."

Sweat is dripping in my eyes when I next open them, and from the bright light in the cave, the sun must be high in the sky. Sarissa has been gone for hours. I pull on the rope, feeling whatever she has tied me to bend a little.

She gave me the chip. A clear sign she doesn't believe she will live. Fury burns through my chest at the thought.

I will not allow her to die this way. Not while I'm still breathing.

"Obstinate, impulsive, stubborn witch." I mutter a litany of curses as I yank on the rope, managing to raise my head to scan the cave for weapons. There—by the remnants of the fire—is a knife. I stretch my foot toward it, but it's too far, and the drug once again pulls me under.

CHAPTER NINE

S arissa

Teriez feeds me freshly cooked udazin, while Urox helps me go over the finer points of my plan.

"You're going to need a bigger impact," he murmurs. "Especially if you're hoping to take down that canopy."

"What do you suggest?"

"Let me think about it. We need the distraction to be so big that most of the Dokhalls are consumed by it...or at least have their attention focused on it."

I nod. "My thoughts exactly."

Teriez holds out her hand for my clean plate. "Thank you," I say. "That was delicious."

My stomach twists at the thought of Korzyn, still in that cave. He must be starving.

"Are you okay?" Teriez asks.

I explain what I was just thinking, and Teriez nods. "We

will give you meat to take with you. The commander won't starve."

"I can pay you—"

Teriez waves that off. "My sister told me all about you and your cousin. She was impressed by you both, and it takes a lot to impress Weva."

She gets to her feet. "Now, I had just heated water for a bath before you arrived. Why don't you take it?"

"Oh no, I couldn't."

"Oh yes, you can."

I blush some more, and Urox laughs. His face clears as I hesitate.

"I can leave the tashiv if you like."

"Huh? Oh no, it's nothing like that...it's just...the commander."

"You feel bad about him lying in his own filth in that cave?"

"He's not lying in his own filth!"

Urox grins, and I realize I took his bait.

I sigh. "I do feel bad about it, yes."

"Well, look at it this way. I need to go find a few things so we can make sure everything will go smoothly. And only an idiot would hit the Dokhalls during daylight. There's no reason not to bathe."

Well, when he puts it like that. I glance at Teriez. "I'd love a bath, if you're sure it's not too much trouble."

"Not at all."

She leads me into a small bathing room, and guilt hits me at the sight of her bath, still steaming. Hot water is a luxury around here. It must have taken her a long time to heat enough water.

"I'll get you a fresh dress," she says, and I vow to someday repay this family for their help.

I strip off and slide into the water. Teriez returns with a clean gray dress and hands me some soap.

"I'm going to go send a message to our cousin," she says. "She lives in the Seinex Forest—between the cave where your commander is and your camp. Once you've created enough chaos for the Dokhalls, you can get your commander onto a mishua and get to Iprox. She'll give you a place to stay overnight if you need one."

"Thank you. He's not *my* commander, by the way. He's Arix's commander."

Teriez smiles. "A female doesn't fret this much over the well-being of a male unless he is hers."

I wrestle with that while Teriez leaves to send her message. I can see how she'd get the wrong idea about Korzyn and me. But it's just basic loyalty. I'd worry about anyone I'd left alone in that cave.

I chew on my lip. Maybe I should've waited. But if the Dokhalls had found us in that cave, we would've been in big trouble. At least this way, we have a chance of slowing them down so we can get back to camp.

I dunk my head and scrub my hair. The water turns a light brown, and I wince. Gross.

I'm drying myself and reaching for the clean dress when Teriez returns. Her smile makes the corners of her dark eyes crinkle as she runs her gaze over me.

"Well, you look cleaner."

"I feel like a new woman."

Her gaze lingers on my lower legs, and she gasps. "That looks painful."

I shrug. "Thanks for the bath."

She waves that off and leads me back to the fire, handing me a comb for my hair. I manage to work through most of the knots and tie it back in a braid while we wait for Urox.

A braid...

I turn to Teriez. "I have an idea." I tell her what I need, and she nods, leading me out of her house and to the forest. She stops and points to the long, dry branches of a tree that's similar to a weeping willow on Earth, only the branches are much thicker and stronger. I run my finger along one of them and smile. Perfect.

I climb the tree, knife in hand, and slice through the long leaves so Teriez can catch them below me. She cocks her head, and I grin at her as I shuffle and slide back down the tree.

We drag the branches through the back of the forest and behind Teriez's house—away from prying eyes. Then I sit outside in the afternoon sun and braid the branches into a rope.

It certainly isn't pretty, but hopefully it'll work for what I need.

When I'm done, Teriez offers me more food, but I'm too nervous to eat, my stomach tangled in knots as I sit back down near her fire.

The sun is going down when Urox arrives, taking off his boots at the door.

"I found the pods," he says. "Are you ready?"

"Ready as I'll ever be. Listen, I have an idea, but I'm scared the fire will get out of control and burn everything to the ground."

Urox smiles at me. "You'll find that the trees in this part of the forest are remarkably resilient. Their leaves may burn, but it would have to be an extremely hot fire to damage their trunks."

I raise my eyebrow at that. "What if it spreads to the town?"

"Did you happen to notice the charred ground between the river and this forest?"

I smile. A natural firebreak. Thanks, Dragix. The dragon may not have been around when I needed to use him as a flying taxi, but he's proving helpful after all.

"And on the other side?"

"An open plain between this forest and the Seinex Forest. You'll likely remember crossing it when you were on your way to the Colossal Water last time."

He gives me a dismissive wave of his hand, and I narrow my eyes. That's the exact gesture I make when I'm about to start some shit. Urox is clearly looking for some action.

"What exactly do you do for a living anyway?"

He grins. "I'd tell you, but I'd have to ensure you could no longer speak any secrets to anyone."

That sounds a lot like "I'd tell you, but I'd have to kill you." And that's *my* line.

I shrug it off. "All righty then. Let's get this party started."

Korzyn

My heart pounds as I search through the forest for the little hellion. She is small, and from the struggle in her quarters, it's clear she is bleeding. Whoever took her will not need her for long. Just long enough to ensure her cousin cooperates.

I curse. If she had trusted me, perhaps I could have helped her.

I ignore the little voice in my head that insists she was right not to trust me. She is loyal to her fellow human females, and I am loyal to my king. Neither of us have room for anything else.

I break into a run. Her captors didn't have time to take her far. With every entrance and exit to the castle monitored for the banquet, the only way they could have gotten her out is through one of the not-so-secret passageways, through the garden, and into the forest.

Unless they somehow managed to smuggle her into a hydro and down the river.

Or they've already killed her.

Why do my hands fist at the thought? She is a human female—nothing to me.

Footsteps sound, and I draw my sword, frowning at the pained gasps breaking the silence of the forest. I move away from the main path and almost collide with Sarissa.

I stare at her, the relief overwhelming. She's covered in dirt, with a bruise on her cheek and blood dripping down her arm.

"Of course it would be you," she mutters, and I shake myself.

"Why am I not surprised that you're bleeding and running through our forest?"

She smiles at that, and I can't help but stare.

The forest fades around me.

I'm watching as she dances with one of the guards, an honorable male who I would trust at my back. She twines her arms around his neck, smiling up at him, and I grit my teeth.

"Commander?"

A beautiful female is offering me a cup of noptri, and I take a deep gulp. She raises one elegant eyebrow, her eyes dark and fathomless.

"Something wrong?"

I smile at her, and she blushes under my attention—a demure female.

"Nothing is wrong," I murmur. "In fact, many things just became right."

Her blush deepens, and I smile, charmed.

"Would you like to dance?"

She nods, and I spin her around the dance floor until Arix announces that Seva has begun. The female talks of trivial things and court gossip I have no interest in. Her laugh is light, however, and her dress is cut in a way that pleases the eye. It's dark, form-fitting, and not at all like the crimson dress worn by the hellion, still grinning up at my guard.

I hadn't realized he was so amusing.

"I will go get a cloak," the female says. "Meet me outside?"

"Of course."

I find a secluded corner, realizing I don't know the female's name. I shrug, staring up at the shooting stars. I will ask her name, and perhaps I will tumble her this night. Maybe it will take the edge off the emptiness.

I pull my eyes from the sky as the female sits down, her cloak wrapped securely around her. She sighs up at the stars, for once not speaking, simply enjoying the moment.

When she leans into me, I'm hit with a bolt of lust, and when her lips touch mine, I find a part of me that has long been missing.

Laughter breaks the moment, and the female rears back. I frown, but she seems to feel suddenly shy as she gets to her feet, rushing away.

I stand, trailing her through the crowd, but she's gone.

I toss my head, feeling the hard ground beneath me. I need to get out of this cave. Need to go after the female.

She leans over me, tears in her eyes.

"If I don't come back, tell the other women I'm sorry. Tell Vivian...tell her I went out with a knife in my hand." She smiles, but it's sad. "And tell them all to have good lives. Lives they'll be proud of." It's Sarissa's lips on mine now, the kiss somehow apologetic, hinting at regret.

She walks away, her feet thudding on the cave floor with each step.

"Don't you dare leave me," I roar, pulling at the rope.

I come awake as my hands hit me in the stomach. The rope holding them snaps, and I let out a growl of relief.

I sit up, and the cave lurches around me, but I reach for some water, gulping it down. It's dark, and the thudding wasn't Sarissa's footsteps at all. In the distance, something is exploding.

I close my eyes. What has the minx done now?

I manage to get to my feet, swiping up my sword on the way. My steps are surprisingly sure as I make it out of the cave. How long have I been asleep?

I untie the mishua, and she snorts. "I know you're hungry," I murmur. "So am I. But we need to go find my hellion."

***

Sarissa

BOOM.

I grin from my hiding spot next to a huge tree. On the other side of the Dokhalls' camp, Urox has started his part of the plan. Both of us insisted that Teriez stay behind—me because I don't want to be responsible for anyone else getting hurt, and Urox because he said she had no stomach for death.

The Dokhalls do exactly what most people would do in this situation. They panic. Most of them run south, away from the explosions, many of them changing direction when Urox lets another pod loose on the west side of their camp.

But the biggest threats will be running toward the explosions. They'll be sent to neutralize whoever is threatening the camp.

I blow out a long, nervous breath. I hope Urox is safe. Truthfully, he seems like an adrenaline junkie who's finally getting a fix.

I'm happy to be able to help him with that.

I wait until most of the Dokhalls have cleared out around this part of the camp, and then I loop the rope around my arm again and again until it's no longer dragging on the ground.

The climb is tough. I usually have pretty good upper-body strength, but after climbing so many trees, my hands are covered in cuts and blisters.

I aim for a branch that's high enough to get the job done but sturdy enough that it looks like it's unlikely to snap under my weight.

Don't look down.

I focus above my head instead, at the canopy of dried dirt and poop that has helped hide these guys from Dragix's eyes—and nose.

On Earth, dried animal dung is used as a fuel source in many countries. From how dry the leaves on this canopy look, that poop has been baking in the Agron sun for days. That means it should be highly flammable.

I reach my branch and take a seat, one hand clutching at the tree above me. Sweat begins to drip into my eyes, and I lean my face down, wiping my forehead on my arm.

This part of my plan seemed a lot easier in my head.

I pull most of the rope off my other arm and shuffle out along the branch until there's nothing between me and the canopy. Then I begin to swing the rope like a lasso. All I need is for it to hook onto the canopy, and the rest will be easy.

I miss.

And then I miss again.

And again.

More explosions sound from the west—a warning. If I don't hurry this up, the Dokhalls will likely realize Urox is just a distraction and head this way. Or they'll find and kill him.

Stay cool. Panic will get you killed.

I hadn't thought about how hard it would be—not just the physical part, but the smell of the smoke beginning to drift into my nostrils, the crackle of fire in the distance. Memories crawl toward me, tugging at my concentration and urging me to pay attention to them.

I force myself to focus, to stay in the here and now, and to try again.

I get closer to the canopy this time, but it takes me a while to gather the rope again as it falls. I'll try once more, and then I need to move to plan B.

There is no plan B!

I let go of the branch above my head, wobbling danger- ously as I tense the muscles in my stomach and use them to balance. I throw the rope, and this time I manage to get it inches from the canopy above my head before it falls, the weight of it unbalancing me.

I slam my free hand into the side of the tree as the ground spins below me.

That was close.

"What," a low voice growls, "do you think you're doing?"

I turn my head so fast I almost get whiplash. Below me, standing next to my tree, the commander glowers up at me, his teeth bared.

"Korzyn?" I hiss. "What the hell are you doing here? How are you even on your feet?"

He ignores that. "Move."

"What?"

My eyes are glued to his body as he begins his climb. The strain shows on his face, but he makes it close to me, jerking his head in a clear order for me to get out of his way.

Another explosion, this one closer, and I flinch, handing my makeshift rope to Korzyn as he climbs onto a branch higher than mine.

I hold my breath, certain the branch will snap beneath his weight, but he doesn't look concerned.

"Get down on the ground," he says, and I roll my eyes but start climbing down. Someone's still grumpy about being drugged and left in that cave. Such a drama queen.

Hope flutters in my chest as he swings the rope, hooking the end of it in the canopy on his first try.

Show-off.

He's obviously on the same page as me with this plan because he nestles the other end of the rope into a crack between his branch and the tree.

He climbs down until he's eye level with the end of the rope, pulls a coil from his pocket, and holds it against the rope.

I begin moving faster until I can jump down from the tree. I close my eyes at the feel of the ground beneath my feet before opening them at the thud of boots next to me.

Korzyn's face is a mask of cold rage. I open my mouth, but he reaches out, his hand fast as a whip as he buries it in my hair, pulling me to him.

His mouth crashes down on mine, and I go instantly hot all over. His arms surround me, his mouth hard and dominating, and for the first time since I left him in that cave, I feel...safe.

He pulls away, his expression still full of wrath, but his eyes are burning with promise.

"Get on the mishua." He jerks his head behind me, and the moment is gone.

"Urox is in trouble. I'm not done yet."

I reach into the wide pocket of my dress and pull out a pod the size of a small coconut. Korzyn closes his eyes briefly, as if reaching for patience, before opening them and immediately surveying our surroundings. Above us, the canopy catches fire, the crackling sound making me flinch, and Korzyn growls.

"Who's Urox?"

"My contact."

He struggles with that for a moment. "Where?"

"East of here. We need to give him a chance to get away."

"Fine. Get on the mishua."

I don't argue. Korzyn stumbles once on his way to the mishua, and I reach out a hand to steady him before pulling it away as he glowers at me.

He's still weak.

He probably feels like shit.

But he came for me.

CHAPTER TEN

K orzyn

I allow Sarissa to get off the mishua long enough to throw her pod. Despite myself, I smile at the savage grin that spreads across her face as it explodes.

Dokhalls are sprinting in all directions. One of them comes close, and I swing my sword, beheading him before he sees me.

"Nice," Sarissa says, and I grab her hand, pulling her up on the mishua in front of me.

"We leave now."

"I need to go to our meeting point."

I frown. "Who exactly is this contact?"

"Urox is a friend's brother. He put a lot on the line to help us, Korzyn."

I grind my teeth but follow her directions. We wait for a few minutes, and I open my mouth to tell the hellion the male is likely dead.

A half-breed Braxian steps through the trees.

"Thought you weren't going to make that last explosion." He grins at Sarissa, and she grins back.

Their own little private moment. Delightful.

She jerks her head. "Urox, meet Korzyn—the commander. He's the one who threw the rope in the end. Turns out I was overly optimistic about my abilities."

Urox gives her a slow smile. "I wouldn't say that."

Three seconds. I could dispatch him in three seconds. Two if I jumped off the mishua, using her back for leverage.

Sarissa slides down before I can stop her, my mind still visualizing removing the male's head from his body as she strides over to him.

"Thank you so much," she murmurs. "I couldn't have done it without you."

That's enough of that.

"We need to leave," I say, and she glances up at me but nods.

"Anytime." Urox grins at her as if I didn't speak, and I ignore the burning sensation in my chest at the interest in his eyes. "Feel free to come back and visit once all this is over," he says. "A female like you would keep life interesting."

"The hellion is leaving this planet," I say, and Sarissa gives me a dirty look, then shifts her attention back to Urox.

"I'll send you guys a message when I get to Rakiz's camp and we've taken care of the Dokhalls," she promises.

Urox hugs her goodbye, and I grit my teeth. He smiles at me over her shoulder, but the smile falls from his face at whatever he sees in my eyes.

Sarissa steps back, and Urox swings a bundle from over his shoulder, handing it to her.

"Food from Teriez. She said to make sure your

commander eats some meat." He flicks his eyes at me, and I tamp down the urge to tell him exactly what he can do with that food.

"Please thank her for me," Sarissa says. She steps closer to the mishua, and I offer her my hand, pulling her up in front of me. The male meets my gaze, challenge clear on his face, and I bare my teeth. His face hardens, and he gives me a short nod before he turns and walks away.

"What was that about?" Sarissa mutters as I direct the mishua into motion.

"You left me to attack the Dokhalls with a strange male you had never met."

She doesn't look back at me, but I can feel her rolling her eyes. "And?"

"If you don't know why this doesn't please me, then you're not as intelligent as I had imagined."

"You know, you recovered remarkably quickly once you were forced to rest. Those maradoza berries obviously did the trick." She turns her head and smiles sunnily over her shoulder at me. "You're welcome."

I let out a low growl. "Do not believe your actions *helped* me, female."

She sighs. "Korzyn...about that kiss in the cave..."

"Forget it. You believed you were about to die. Emotions were high. Besides, I am still committed to finding my female."

"Your female? You mean the mystery woman you had one kiss with? You sound like a stalker."

I smile. "How do you know it was one kiss?"

"You said it was."

"No, I didn't."

She opens her mouth, but I slap my hand over it as the

mishua goes still beneath us. Sarissa pries my hand off her face but stays silent, both of us waiting for the attack.

We don't have long to wait.

Four Dokhalls surround us, likely one of the scouting groups sent ahead.

Heli lowers her head, horns glinting in the moonlight. One of the Dokhalls waves his stick weapon at us threateningly.

"Dismount," he orders, and I laugh.

"Do not think to tell me what to do," I say, and Sarissa snorts.

"Throw me at that one," she mutters.

I can see her plan, and I tilt my head. "No."

"Divide and conquer," she whispers as the Dokhalls advance toward us. "You have to trust me at some point."

I grind my teeth, but she's right. She has proven she can fight the Dokhalls and prevail.

"Fine."

She pulls up her feet, tucking herself into a ball, and I throw her over the Dokhalls' heads. She lands on her feet, rolls, and rises with a long knife in her hand.

The Dokhalls attack.

Sarissa

Three of the Dokhalls leap at Korzyn, while one of them bares his teeth and jumps at me. I drop and roll out of the way. He falls, immediately turning toward me again, and I wince at him as I get a good look at his horns.

"Already broken one of your horns, huh? That must've hurt."

I glance at Korzyn, who jumps off the mishua and draws his sword, slashing it at one of the Dokhalls. Another attempts to attack at the same time, and Korzyn punches him in the face, swiping his stick from his hand and beating him with it.

"So," he says between blows. "While I am helpless as a babe in that cave, you find another male to attack the Dokhalls?"

I gape at him, narrowly missing being jabbed with Broken Horn's stick. I duck, roll, and slice up with my knife, catching the Dokhall in the thigh.

He howls, falling back, and I jump to my feet.

"It wasn't like that, Korzyn."

"What was it like?"

"I was trying to save you!"

"I believe you mean you were trying to save the females back at your camp."

I glance at him, but he's not looking at me. Instead, he's advancing on the largest Dokhall, who finally has the good sense to look afraid.

Broken Horn attempts to use his stick as a sword, and I dodge, striking out with my fist.

"What do you care? You're only doing this so you can get back to your mystery woman."

He laughs but not like it's funny. "You're right."

Jealousy shoots through me, and I take it out on Broken Horn, slamming my knee into his groin. He groans, dropping his stick as he folds, and I pick it up, smashing it down on his head.

"She can't be that great if you left."

Not only am I jealous of myself, but I'm talking shit about myself too. Awesome.

"It was worth leaving to find her name."

That's it.

The Dokhall rises with a snarl, and I kick him in the face. His eyes roll back in his head, and he hits the ground with a dull thump.

Korzyn's still fighting the largest Dokhall, but it seems as if he's playing with him, smoothly dodging each of his strikes, hammering him with a punch, and then dancing backward.

"I'm the mystery female, you idiot. So you can stop looking!"

His grin is savage, practically radiating pure male arrogance. "I know."

My mouth drops open. "You know?"

He obviously gets tired of taunting the Dokhall because he pulls a knife free, stabbing him in the gut before using his sword to smoothly behead him.

"How could you possibly know? Why would you take this trip if you knew?"

"Oh, I didn't know then. I suspected the moment you kissed me in that cave. And then I had a *very* interesting dream that helped me put it all together. Tasting you again in the forest...well, that just confirmed my suspicions."

His low voice makes something in my stomach clench.

He swipes his sword on the Dokhall's shirt, cleaning the blood off it. Then he narrows his eyes at me, and it's evident he most definitely *doesn't* forgive me for not telling him I was his mystery woman. Or for leaving him in the cave.

Fine, then.

I step toward him until I'm close enough to reach out and remove my earring from his shirt. It's little more than rags at this point, and he's moved the earring from the spot I first placed it to a more secure location, where the material is stronger, between his shoulder and his neck. I meet his eyes, and he stares at me, pulling away once I've slid my earring back into my ear.

Not the most hygienic thing I've ever done, but I'm not taking any more chances.

Korzyn is watching me, likely silently judging each move I make. I sniff and stalk over to the mishua before hauling myself onto her back.

I blink as Korzyn climbs up behind me, a grunt leaving his throat, and I crane my neck.

"Your arm is bleeding."

"It's fine," he rumbles.

Silence is heavy between us for the next few hours.

The commander refuses to stop at Urox's cousin's, and I can't blame him. As much as he needs to rest and recover, both of us are itching to get to Rakiz's camp so we can warn everyone about the Dokhalls.

Besides, asking the paranoid commander who has just been poisoned to spend the night in the home of someone he doesn't know?

Not a good idea.

Now that we're no longer actively fighting, the bitter scent of smoke is making my stomach roil.

I hate the smell of smoke. To me, fire doesn't represent warmth and comfort. It represents death and horror.

No matter what I do, and no matter where I go, there's no escaping one horrific fact.

My sister is dead.

Claire never got to live. She never got any real adventures. And it's all my fault.

We travel all night, and I eventually fall into a light sleep before waking up with my head resting against Korzyn's chest. He doesn't comment when I move away, blinking at the wide plain in front of us.

I can no longer smell smoke, so I hope that means the fire is no longer raging through that forest.

"Can I ask you something?"

The commander hesitates, and I can practically feel him radiating suspicion. "Yes."

"Where's your family?"

He tenses behind me. "I'm from a tribe on the outskirts of Heriast. When the king and queen were murdered, Arix needed a guard with no political ties or aspirations. One from a family that was unknown at court, with no history, no weaknesses that could be used for bribery or blackmail." He shrugs. "I was well known in my tribe for my strength and speed with a sword."

He doesn't say it like he's proud. He says it as if he... regrets his talent.

"How old were you when you left your tribe?"

"I had seen fourteen summers."

"So young."

He shrugs again. "I was larger than most males my age. Besides, I had to be trained...molded into a guard that could protect Arix with his life."

"So you were all alone? With no family?"

"Yes. So was Arix. He had his uncle, but we were unable to trust him, given that he would be next in line for the throne if Arix was murdered."

I keep my eyes on the horizon as I think about what he's said. A few hundred feet in front of us, the forest beckons, leading us back toward Rakiz's tribe.

"Do you have siblings?"

He shrugs. "My mother was pregnant when I left. I don't know how many children she had after me."

My heart twists in my chest for him.

"Do you see your family now?"

"No."

The word is a low growl, and I drop the subject.

When he realizes I'm not going to pry, he seems to relax, leaning back in the saddle.

"And your family?" he asks.

"I don't see them either."

"Why?"

"I had a sister, and she died."

The smell of smoke, thick in my nostrils, choking off my air. The flames, dancing so close, and my voice, turning hoarse as I scream for Claire...

"Hellion?"

I shake it off. "When she died, I couldn't look at my parents, and they couldn't look at me. I left." I smile, but it feels fake on my face. "I guess we've got that in common."

We're silent as we enter the forest, both of us brooding. I know I'll have nightmares tonight.

They say some memories are ghosts of your past. Mine are zombies. There's nothing that can stop them when they come for me.

By the time we reach the first sentries close to Rakiz's camp, Korzyn is slumping behind me. To be honest, I'm still stunned he made it to me, given he could barely move when I left him.

The sentry is one I recognize, and he nods at us, letting us through. The next sentry stares at us, eyes wide, and I realize we must look like we've been through some shit.

I'm covered in dirt from our fight and wearing a dress I cut off at the knees so I could fight. Korzyn stripped off his shirt and had a quick wash in a stream when we stopped to refill our water, but other than that, he hasn't bathed in days and his clothes are little more than rags.

"Sarissa?"

We've made it to the camp gates, and I grin at Zoey, who runs toward us, concern in her eyes. "What happened to you guys?"

We dismount, and Korzyn puts out a hand to steady me as my legs wobble. He's turning gray, and it's evident he needs to lie down.

I send him an *"Are you okay?"* look, and he ignores me.

Fine.

I give Zoey a rundown of the last few days as we walk toward Rakiz's tashiv.

"You haven't seen Dragix either?" Zoey chews on her lower lip.

"No. If he was anywhere near that forest, he would've seen the smoke and likely come to investigate."

"He's been gone for days," Zoey says in a low voice. "Charlie is a wreck. She's convinced that a group of Zintas managed to hide their scent from him long enough to build some kind of trap."

Dread sits heavy in my stomach.

Korzyn clears his throat behind me. "Which direction did he fly when he left?"

Zoey points, and Korzyn nods. "It's likely he's still hunting to the northeast, then. We came from the west. It's not surprising we haven't seen him."

It's still bad news that he hasn't returned. Dragix never would've left his pregnant mate for this long without communicating if he wasn't in trouble. But a tiny part of my heart melts at Korzyn's attempt at reassurance.

I freeze as a strange furred animal stalks closer.

"Don't move," I snap at Zoey, and her eyes widen. I pull my knife, and Zoey slowly turns her head.

She laughs and then glances back at my face. "Don't mind the beastie. His name is Harry."

Harry has sharp teeth, which he bares at me, but after Zoey scolds him, the furred creature prowls close enough for me to pet, nudging my hand when I stroke his ears.

We've traveled all night, and it's not yet dawn. While Rakiz will need to be woken, I'm tamping down my urge to wake up Alexis and give her the chip. That would be a dick move, even if I am desperate to hand it over.

Rakiz has obviously already been informed about our arrival because he opens the door to his tashiv himself, waving us in.

He glances toward his bedroom door and raises one finger to his lips, signaling that Nevada and Danica are sleeping. I'll keep this quick.

"We were waiting for Dragix to arrive. When he didn't, we left Heriast to bring the chip back here. But someone poisoned our food. While the commander was recovering, we found a camp of Dokhalls who had managed to hide their scent from Dragix."

Rakiz's expression is terrible. "How far?"

I glance at Korzyn, who gives Rakiz the directions he needs.

"We set fire to the canopy, and the camp was in chaos when we left. That might slow them down for a while, but it may also spur them into action. They know we know they're there now. If I were their commander, I'd order them to immediately march on your camp."

"There's another thing," I say. "The Dokhalls had set up a trap on the main road leading from the mishua pen on this side of the water. If Arix comes through with his army, they'll be spotted and attacked. They won't kill them all—Arix has a large army, and they're brutal. But it'll probably be enough to slow them down."

Rakiz lets out a low growl, the only sign of his rage, and then his expression turns thoughtful.

"We have been planning to tell the Dokhalls they can have the ship," he says. "This way, the word will spread, and instead of dealing with multiple attacks over a long period of time, we will take them all out at once." The tribe king turns to pace, then glances out his window, his eyes hard as he watches his camp. "We need to spread the message so that all Dokhalls know about it—not just those at the camp you found. That way, we'll be able to hold them off for a few more days as other groups gather forces. It's likely they'll engage in a struggle for power."

Korzyn rubs his hand over his face. "I believe some of the Dokhalls have made alliances with the Zintas and Voildi in exchange for a place on the ship. They'll soon learn there are too many Dokhalls still alive and wanting to get back to their planet—and the ship is unlikely to be big enough to take them all."

I tilt my head. "You guys think some of the Zintas and Voildi will abandon the Dokhalls?"

Rakiz smiles. "I have been making friendships and alliances on this side of the Colossal Water for many years, and yet I still have to be my most charming self when dealing with our Braxian allies. Each interaction involves give and take—strategic moves where each of our tribes feels as if they have won something. The Dokhalls have split into multiple groups, each with a different leader. Now they will have to work together. It will give us more time to make arrangements."

I clear my throat. "One problem. Why would the Dokhalls believe we'd hand over the ship? We've been actively guarding it from them this whole time."

"That's a question Zoey and her friends began

pondering back when Nevada was kidnapped. We believed we might one day need to gather all the Dokhalls into one place, so we allowed rumors to spread about my fury at my mate's kidnapping and how I was no longer willing to protect the females under my care—or the ship itself."

I stare at him. "That's genius," I breathe.

Rakiz nods. "I am," he says, and I laugh. His expression turns serious. "We need to summon our allies."

"And we need to get a message to Arix," Korzyn says. "He needs to be ready for the attack."

My heart pounds in my chest. If I know my cousin, she'll insist on coming with her mate. Vivian's face flashes before my eyes, so still and pale as she lay in a coma for days after Arix was betrayed.

I can't handle the thought of something happening to her.

Someone knocks lightly on the door, and Rakiz opens it.

Terex glances at us and then back to Rakiz. "What do you need?"

"Messengers." Rakiz scans us. "Arrange for kradis for Sarissa and Korzyn and then have four of our strongest warriors sent to me."

Terex nods, and I barely notice as he leaves, my mind foggy with exhaustion.

"We need Dragix," I murmur. "If he can clear the way, Arix can get here faster."

Rakiz sighs. "Once Arix banned any Zintas from his side of the water from allying with the Dokhalls, they had to make a choice. Some of them were lured into an alliance with the Dokhalls simply because they want the chance to board the ship with the Dokhalls and travel to a new planet."

I snort. "If they believe the Dokhalls will hold up their end of that bargain, I've got a bridge I can sell them."

Rakiz's brow creases at that, and he shrugs. "While the Dokhalls are a threat, the Zintas are able to provide them with information they would find extremely helpful. Dragix has been hunting a pack of Zintas that allied with the Dokhalls and then went north, planning to attack Tecar's tribe."

"When did he leave?" Korzyn asks.

"Nine nights ago."

I wince. No wonder Charlie is freaking out. Since Dragix realized she was pregnant, he's been even more overprotective, refusing to leave her side for more than a few hours at a time. Nine nights must have felt like an eternity.

The door opens, and Terex nods at Rakiz, gesturing for us to follow him. I mumble good night to the tribe king and trail after the huge warrior.

Korzyn murmurs something to Rakiz before following us, and we walk in silence until Terex points to Korzyn's kradi.

The commander gives me a look I can't quite read before nodding at Terex and stepping into his kradi.

The sun is beginning to rise in the cloudless emerald sky, the hazy glow of light dancing across the roofs of the kradis.

"I will have Ellie bring you a dress from one of the other females," Terex says. "She is an early riser now."

His eyes turn cloudy, and my throat tightens at the frustration on his face. I haven't been on this planet for long, but one thing I've learned? There's nothing more difficult for a Braxian male than to be unable to help his mate if she's struggling. The Braxians' protective instincts seem to be continually in overdrive when it comes to their mates.

"How is she doing?"

He shrugs. "The babe is still not here. Moni is insisting it isn't too big for Ellie to birth it, but my little mate is small."

"Human women give birth to surprisingly large babies on Earth," I say, and he nods.

"That is what Zoey says."

He stops at my kradi, and a woman I haven't met ducks out of it, a large empty bucket in her hands.

"I have arranged for baths to be drawn for you and the commander," he says.

"I could kiss you."

The ghost of a smile plays around his mouth, and a tiny bit of the strain on his face disappears. "I don't believe Ellie would like that."

I laugh. "Nope. Good night, Terex."

He glances up at the sun and then grins at me. "Good night."

CHAPTER ELEVEN

S arissa

The kradi is quiet...almost lonely. For the first time in days, I'm by myself, without any plans running through my mind.

The bath calls to me, and I strip off, removing the earring from my ear, and slide into the water with a sigh. I'm so tired I'm worried that if I close my eyes, I'll fall asleep in the bath, so I force myself to dunk my head, scrub every inch of my body, and get out, wrapping one of the long cloths the tribe use as towels around me and then leaning over to wring out my hair in the bath.

"Sarissa?"

"Come in," I call, smiling at Ellie. "You didn't have to get up for me," I say, and she rolls her eyes.

"Don't worry." She runs her hand over her bump. "I was already up."

"How are you feeling?"

"Huge. I know you've only been gone for a few weeks

since Beth's mating ceremony, but it feels like it's been months."

"You poor thing."

She smiles. "This little guy or girl will be worth it. I've always wanted to be a mother. How's Vivian doing?"

"Ruling with an iron fist."

She laughs, and I grin as she hands me a dress. I recognize it as one Vivian wore often when she was here.

"She had her coronation. I can't tell you how weird it was seeing an actual crown on my cousin's head."

"I bet. And you? How are you doing, Sarissa?"

I shrug, picking my earring off the floor and showing it to her. "I have the chip."

I slide it into my ear, and Ellie nods, her eyes steady on my face. "That's great. But how are *you* doing?"

I open my mouth, and my throat suddenly tightens. My eyes dart, and Ellie gives me a sympathetic look.

"Listen to me prying into your personal life. You're exhausted. We can talk later once you've had some rest."

She rubs my arm and smiles at me before waddling out of the kradi as I pull on my dress, unsure why I'm suddenly so upset.

My mission is complete. I've brought the chip back, just like I wanted.

So why am I not jumping for joy?

Maybe I'm just tired.

I wonder if Korzyn has had his arm looked at. Something tells me he's not the type to go to the healers unless someone drags him there.

It's none of your business what the commander does.

I picture him lying in bed, teeth clenched in pain, his arm throbbing. What if he gets an infection?

That's it.

I stride out of my kradi, making my way to the healers' one. Zoey is murmuring to Moni, one of the healers who provided me with a salve that's meant to loosen up my scars.

Zoey glances at me and smiles, finishing up her conversation and making her way toward me. She looks content and completely at home here, and I attempt to shove down the envy that twists my stomach.

"Sarissa, you haven't slept yet? You look exhausted."

I smile. "I'll go to bed soon. Hey, did the commander come by at some point?"

She shakes her head. "I've been here since shortly after you arrived. Couldn't sleep. How come?"

"He took a nasty slice to his arm. It needs to be dressed, but he's likely so stubborn that he'll ignore it and then attempt to fix it himself when it doesn't heal properly." I roll my eyes, and Zoey laughs.

She reaches for a salve on her workbench and hands it to me, along with a handful of bandages. "Give it a clean and then that salve should do the trick. I'd offer him a tonic for the pain, but something tells me he wouldn't take it."

"Nope. Thanks."

"Anytime."

The sun may have just risen, but the camp is already coming to life. Babies are crying, their mothers soothing them, kids are negotiating playing outside, and families are laughing together over their morning meals as I walk between a row of kradis.

I ring the kradi bells.

"Yes?"

The commander's voice is low, almost hoarse, and I hate myself for the way it makes my stomach flutter.

"It's me."

Splashing. Good God, he's in the bath. I don't wait for him to reply. "I'll come back later."

His laugh is a low challenge. "Enter."

I grit my teeth. Another game. If he thinks he'll turn me into a drooling fool just because he happens to be naked, he can think again.

I push through his kradi entrance and come to a halt as silver eyes meet mine.

He's obviously just washed his hair because water is dripping down his face, along the smooth line of his throat, caressing the muscles of the best chest on Agron.

Stop staring, dummy.

His eyes laugh at me as I grind my teeth, stepping closer.

"I noticed you were favoring your left arm. It doesn't make you weak to go to the healers, you know."

He lifts it from the water, and we both examine the deep cut. Blood oozes out, and I let out a growl.

"Are you trying to get an infection?"

"It was dirty. It needed to be cleaned."

His tone is suggestive, and I heroically manage to fight back a blush. I stare him down. It'll take more than that to make me uncomfortable.

Yeah, right. So why are you sweating, hmm?

The corner of his mouth lifts, and he moves. I clamp my eyes shut, ignoring his low laugh as he gets to his feet. From the sound of things, he's drying himself off, and I gulp, wishing I could fan my face.

"You can open your eyes," he murmurs, and I jump.

He's standing inches away, and I clear my throat again.

"If you sit down, I'll be able to reach."

He gives the salve in my hand a look of distaste, and I wave it at him.

"It's an antiseptic."

He sighs. "Fine."

He takes a seat, the towel parting to reveal one huge muscled thigh.

Don't look down.

I jump at the touch of his hand on mine, and I realize he's reaching for the salve. He smiles, looking far too pleased with himself, as he places it on the table next to him.

Silence.

"Hold out your arm."

He complies, and I use one of the bandages to gently spread the salve along the cut. He hisses, and I wince.

"Serves you right for not paying attention."

I know when he got this cut. It was right after I admitted I was his mystery woman.

From the frown on his face, he's thinking the same thing.

"How are you feeling now?"

"Better. I've regained most of my energy. That disgusting water you forced on me saved my life."

I let out a pleased hum as I wrap a bandage around his bicep before tying it off. I pull my hand away, and he catches it in his.

We stare at each other, the crackle of his fire the only noise in his kradi.

Fuck it.

I lean down, and he meets me halfway, his mouth hard on mine. The commander kisses as if every kiss is his last, with a kind of desperate urgency that makes my thighs clench.

His hands cup my head, holding me to him as his tongue presses against my lips, demanding entrance. I open for him, and he sweeps into my mouth with a growl, making me tremble with need.

He pulls me close until I'm straddling him, and I groan at the feel of him so hard and thick beneath me.

Turns out the commander is packing. He moves his lips to my neck, trailing down my skin, and my eyes flutter shut as I sigh against him.

Korzyn's low laugh makes me jolt, and I blink open my eyes as I stare at him. I've never seen him look so...happy before. Tiny lines are crinkled next to his eyes, which glow silver with satisfaction. His full lips are curled into a smile, and I reach out, tracing that smile in an attempt to memorize what it looks like.

"Why did you stop?"

Am I slurring?

"You fell asleep against me. Should I be offended?"

"Did not."

His smile widens into a full-fledged grin. "You snored."

He gets to his feet, holding me easily in his arms despite his injury. I expect him to let me slide down to the ground, but instead, he walks me to the furs in the corner of the kradi, placing me down on them.

"What are you doing?"

"You need to sleep."

My eyes widen at that. And they widen even more as he ditches the towel, crawling under the furs next to me.

"Um."

"You came to me," Korzyn says. "You sleep with me."

"Uh—"

"Close your eyes."

I feel like I should argue my point, but he hauls me into his arms, and he's so warm next to me, and I feel so safe that I...do.

Korzyn

It has been many years since I woke up next to a female. And never did I imagine I would wake up next to this one.

Sarissa...cuddles.

I never would have expected it from the prickly female, but she is slumped over my chest like a baby karja, her claws tucked away as she nuzzles my chest and lets out a tiny snore.

Something uncomfortably like contentment makes my lips curl.

Then I frown. I must not forget this female is a deceiver. A cunning little liar who can't be trusted.

And yet she is also fiercely loyal. I've seen it in her every interaction—even when she had the chance to be rid of me while I was dying in that cave.

Sarissa stretches, a purr leaving her throat, and her nipples rub against my chest.

I grit my teeth. I'm harder than I have ever been, my cock aching as she nestles closer, the wet heat of her suddenly right where I need her.

"Sarissa."

"Mmm." She grinds on me, and I see stars.

"I won't tumble you while you're still asleep," I grit out.

She sighs against my chest, the warm air blowing gently against one of my nipples, and my abs clench.

I once told Arix about the thixis, an animal that lives in the Seinex Forest. It's a small, unassuming animal that would make perfect prey for any predators that hunted it.

But it has a bulb in the back of its throat. With one exhale, the predator becomes a meek, obedient creature.

Sarissa has more in common with a thixis than I ever imagined.

I bury my hand in her hair and pull, just enough to lift her head off my chest.

"Sarissa. Wake. Up."

"Mmm." She blinks open her eyes, which are still blurred with sleep, and I can't help it; I take her mouth, enjoying the low laugh that leaves her throat.

"I was having the dirtiest dream," she murmurs, grinding against me. "Spoiler alert, you featured heavily."

It has been a long time since I have been with a female. Which must be why I'm struggling not to spill against Sarissa's soft thighs.

I pull her closer, taking her mouth once more. She softens against me in a way that's wholly unexpected for the vicious female and yet incredibly erotic. A male who takes this female to his bed knows she would bend only for him and just enough to keep him obsessed with her for the rest of his life.

Ring, ring, ring.

Distantly, I can hear someone ringing the kradi bells. I ignore them, and Sarissa does the same.

"Sarissa?" a voice calls.

She groans, tearing her mouth away from mine, frustration clear on her face.

"Yes?"

"It's Alexis." The voice is full of suppressed laughter. "Ellie said you were back with the chip, so I went to your kradi..." Her voice trails off, and Sarissa seems to come back to herself, blinking at me.

She tenses, glancing around, as if realizing she's in my kradi. With me.

My hands fist, and I force myself not to reach for her as she rolls away, gathering her clothes.

"I'll be right there," she calls, fumbling with her dress. I get to my feet, and Sarissa's gaze drops below my waist. I suppress a laugh at her choked inhalation, and her cheeks turn red.

I step behind her, tying her dress. "We're not done," I murmur in her ear, and she shivers. Alexis's appearance has reminded me that the female will leave this planet as soon as she is able. But she will not leave without feeling me moving deep within her.

My need for her body changes nothing. She started something with our kiss beneath the stars. And now I will finish it.

I may have mistakenly thought she would be my mate when I kissed her that night under the stars, but that changes nothing.

I *will* have her before she leaves.

CHAPTER TWELVE

S arissa

I didn't have any nightmares last night, which, after talking about my family yesterday, was wholly unexpected.

Instead, I had a burning-hot sex dream, starring the commander himself.

It must have been because I was so exhausted.

Are you sure it wasn't because of the commander's arms... and how good those arms felt around you all night?

Yup, I'm positive.

I ignore the snarky voice in my head that calls me a liar as I follow Alexis to the clearing where all of the human women in this camp usually gather as a group.

"Ellie and I didn't say anything." She smiles over her shoulder at me. "Nevada knows, of course, but we wanted to let you be the one to tell everyone."

For one absurd moment, I think she's referring to my morning grind against the commander.

I realize she's waiting. She's talking about the chip. Duh.

I take the earring out of my ear. "Awesome, thanks."

I can hear the other women before I see them, the sounds of gossip and laughter echoing through the camp.

I pull the glass jewel out of my earring and let out a sigh of relief when the silver chip glints at me in the sunlight.

The clearing goes silent as soon as I appear. I don't waste any time, simply holding the tiny chip up to the light. Heads crane, and I'm instantly surrounded by women who are whooping and hollering. Some are sobbing, while others have tears steadily dripping down their cheeks. Clara is laughing incredulously, while Aria does a little boogie, shaking her butt as she winks at me.

Alexis is standing close by, and I hand her the chip. With that simple act, a huge weight has been lifted off my shoulders.

I've done my part. Now it's up to her and Kate to see if the chip will work.

Nevada appears next to me, Danica in her arms. I grin at both of them, running a hand over Danica's soft head.

"Nice work, Rissa," Nevada says, and I smile. From Nevada, that's glowing praise.

She lets the other women chat excitedly for a few more minutes, and then she hands Danica over to me with a wink.

I smile down at the baby, who blinks up at me while sucking on her thumb. "Joke's on your mommy," I coo. "I was hoping for a Dani cuddle."

Nevada grins back at me before stepping up on a large rock. She puts two fingers to her mouth and lets out a piercing whistle.

I glance down at Danica, but she's completely unconcerned.

I sway with her in my arms. "Between your warrior

father and your fearless mother, you've got some baller genes, kid."

The women give Nevada their attention, and her face sobers.

"Okay," she says. "We have the chip." She smiles as the other women cheer. "Yes, that's all thanks to Sarissa's determination and gung ho attitude. And her sexy commander, of course."

The other women crack up as I groan. "He's not *my* commander," I mutter, but Nevada ignores that.

"But the chip is just the first step. Alexis and Kate need to get onto the ship to see if the chip will work. I don't have to explain exactly how dangerous that is. They'll be heading to the ship tomorrow, under full guard, and if the Braxians agree it's safe enough to get on the ship, they'll let us know if the chip is usable. They'll also do some analysis to see if the ship can actually be flown out of here. In the meantime, we have bigger problems."

The clearing goes silent, all signs of celebration gone.

"War is coming. And it's coming soon."

Nevada explains everything, from the trap the Dokhalls set for anyone crossing the water, to the camp—and our attempt to set it all aflame.

"They know they're no longer hidden, which means their plans are in high gear. They don't know we have the chip, but I have little doubt their spies will find out soon. We need to prepare."

She glances at Ivy, who nods, stepping forward.

"I've created a schedule of tasks that need to be completed. These include everything from sorting and building weapons to reinforcing the camp gates and taking stock of our food levels. If you're not sure where your skills will be best used, ask."

Nevada nods in agreement. "Believe me, there's something for everyone."

One of the younger women, a teenager called Lace, raises her hand. "How long do we have?"

I've always liked Lace. A few days after we landed—before we realized we'd need the control chip to use the ship—Nevada and a bunch of the other women had a meeting. They worried about allowing the younger women to get on the ship. After all, many of them were under the age of eighteen, and as Clara argued, you can't even enlist for the military in the USA until you're seventeen. Were they really mature enough to make the decision to go to space on such a risky journey?

Amongst the women who landed with me, there are five or six teenagers, ranging in age from fifteen to nineteen. Teenagers are tough, and so far, the younger women have rolled with the punches, fitting in well with the Braxians their age.

But not Lace.

She refuses to hang out with the other kids unless they're training. She has an aptitude for fighting, and when I asked her about her past, the hard look in her eyes made me shut my mouth.

She argued passionately with Clara, stating the teenagers had been through more than anyone could have expected at that age and insisting life experience should count for something. She swore she would be on that ship no matter what Clara said and pointed out Clara wasn't her parent.

"You're sliding perilously close to 'you're not the boss of me,'" Nevada said. "Quit while you're ahead."

Lace stared Nevada down before finally turning and stomping away.

"Unless you're asking us to chain her up, she's going with you," Nevada said, and Clara got a steely look in her eye. I have no doubt Clara is planning something that will have Lace mysteriously detained when it's time for us to leave. But I'm also sure Lace can take anything Clara throws out.

"For what it's worth," I said, "I think you should take her. Who are we to tell her it's not safe when we're about to do the exact same trip?"

"We're informed," Hannah piped up. "Hence why many of us are choosing to stay here. When you're that age, you think you're invincible."

Ivy slowly shook her head. "No," she said. "Not if you've been abducted by aliens and crashed on a strange planet. You don't think you're invincible at all. In fact, you know down to your bones that any illusion of safety can be stolen from you without any warning."

Danica's fist hits me in the face, and I realize I'm daydreaming. I've still only had a few hours' sleep, and despite myself, all I want to do is go back to Korzyn's kradi and curl up next to him.

Oh, please. You want to do a lot more than that.

"Sarissa?"

"Hmm? Oh. I don't think we damaged their army as much as we'd hoped. They may not have that poop canopy to hide under anymore, but unless Dragix flew over after us and torched all of them, they're likely regrouping and making plans."

The crowd goes silent, and all eyes turn to Charlie, who's sitting on a rock on the edge of the clearing. Her shoulders are hunched, and she looks heartsick, her face pale and drawn.

Good one, Sarissa. Why don't you kick her while she's down while you're at it?"

"Okay," Nevada says, drawing all eyes back to her. Charlie seems to pay no attention, staring into space. I glance at Zoey, who's sitting next to her, and the healer meets my gaze with a nod. She's concerned too.

"We'll meet back here after Alexis and Kate have tried the chip. In the meantime, we all need to get to work."

Nevada turns, taking Danica from my arms. I'd never admit it, but I miss the solid weight of her when she's gone. Nevada pats her on the butt, wipes drool off her chin, and gestures for me to follow her.

"Rakiz is meeting with Dexar and Tecar. I think he'll probably invite your commander to that little club as well. Why don't you come join Ellie and me for lunch?"

My stomach grumbles, and I grin, pushing away thoughts of Korzyn. "Sure."

Ellie is already waiting in Nevada's tashiv when we arrive. "Sorry, guys, I just didn't have it in me to go to the meeting."

Nevada shrugs. "You didn't miss anything. If I know Ivy, she'll be delegating tasks right now. Your only task is to have that baby."

Ellie sticks her tongue out at Nevada as she puts her feet up on one of the stools in front of her.

Arana walks into the room, a tray in her arms. She tuts at Nevada. "Now, now," she says. "Remember how desperate you were for Danica to make an appearance."

I laugh as Arana places the tray on the table before turning and taking Danica from Nevada.

"Yes," Nevada says. "And she chose the most inconvenient time possible."

"Babies usually do. Let me spend some time with my favorite while you have lunch."

"Okay. She needs to go down for a nap soon."

Arana waves her hand in an "I got this" motion and waltzes toward Nevada's bedroom.

"Arana is like a second mom to Dani," Nevada tells us. "I don't know what I'd do without her." She waves at the food. "Dig in."

I sit down and load up some fresh bread with meat and some roasted vegetables. Nevada does the same, while Ellie sticks to water.

"I'm not all that hungry. So tell me," Ellie says with a glint in her eye. "How come I found you in the commander's kradi this morning?"

Nevada inhales and chokes, her eyes watering as she has a coughing fit. I sigh, taking another bite of my sandwich while I figure out just how to answer that question.

"We hate each other."

"Yes," Ellie nods seriously. "Most people wake up next to the people they hate."

Nevada recovers from her choking and laughs. "Well, I did."

I stare at her.

"Oh, you didn't know? Rakiz and I loathed each other. I thought he was a stubborn, bossy dictator, and he thought I was a wild, irresponsible menace." She grins. "Turns out we were both right."

"How did I not know this?" For some reason, I thought they must've hit it off the first time they met. After all, they're clearly made for each other.

Nevada shrugs. "By the time you guys arrived, we'd been mated for a while. But we were like oil and water when we first met. I kept trying to sneak out of the camp to find Ivy and the others, and he sentenced me to work in the mishua pen."

"The mishua pen?" My mouth drops open, and she laughs.

Ellie winks at me. "Joke was on him because Nevada befriended his mishua and stole it."

"Wow. I knew you'd stolen a mishua, but I had no idea you were working in the pen or that it was *Rakiz's* mishua."

Ellie rolls her eyes. "She enjoyed working in that pen; don't let her tell you any different."

I tilt my head at that, and Nevada curls her arm, showing off impressive biceps. "I got to work on these. Anyway, enough about me. I thought you hated that commander."

"I do. And he hates me too. We just have…"

"Insane, explosive chemistry?" Nevada suggests, and Ellie sniggers.

"That's about right."

"I think you should go for it," Ellie says. "Braxians are fun." She wiggles her eyebrows, and Nevada stares at her.

"I don't even recognize you anymore." She turns back to me. "Look, I'm not gonna clam jam you, but I think you should be careful. Many a smart, capable woman has been derailed by these warriors. If you're serious about getting on that ship, have your fun but keep your heart out of it."

I snort. "Oh, don't you worry, my heart is nowhere near it."

Nevada gives me a long look, and then a slow smile spreads over her face. "Yeah," she says. "That's what I thought when I met Rakiz."

Korzyn

There are some people in this universe who glow, drawing others to them instinctively. Few of them notice they do it—and many would deny it if one pointed it out.

Sarissa is one of these people.

I first noticed it when I would follow her to and from the marketplace and through the town near Arix's castle, keeping an eye on her. She has an uncanny ability to make people trust her. To make them want to befriend her.

I once heard Vivian ask her why she was so successful at making contacts. She replied she was trained to win others over so she could get the information she needs.

I vowed to never tell her anything, but Sarissa didn't attempt to befriend me. Likely because she knew I'd see through her.

It's not that she's cunning, sneaky, or deceptive—although she's all these things. It's that she also seems to genuinely care for others, in spite of herself.

Often, she'll be walking through this camp alone, clearly deep in thought. Within moments, one of her friends will join her, inviting her to eat with them. Or a younger female will come to her, lip trembling until Sarissa throws an arm around her shoulders.

The children sit on her knees. The babies go quiet in her arms, staring up at her. Even some of the older Braxian males have been known to stop bickering when she glances their way.

I'm slowly learning this prickly female. She frowns at me from across the training arena, where she's currently helping Nevada teach a group of the younger women to fight with a knife.

I smile at her, and she looks confused for a moment,

glancing away when one of the other females calls her name.

The more I watch her, the more I understand.

Sarissa needs harmony. She needs to be needed, and she feels as if her place in the universe is in front of those weaker than herself. That's why she promised the females they would have their revenge. Because she knew she would sacrifice herself to get them their vengeance.

But who sacrifices for Sarissa?

"If you stare any harder, that female will likely make her displeasure known," a voice says, and I glance to my left.

Dexar leans on the fence, a smile on his face as he watches his own mate train with a crossbow.

"I'm thinking."

Dexar raises his eyebrow. "Clearly. You know, you're running out of time to make her yours."

"She's not mine."

"Not yet."

"She's leaving."

His smile grows wider, and he winks at his mate as she turns her head, grinning at him. Envy makes my neck itch.

"Every single one of our human mates thought they were leaving," he says. "We were enough to make them stay. Are you enough to make her stay?"

He walks away, but I already know my answer.

No. I wasn't enough to make my parents keep me. Wasn't enough to even be allowed to visit. This female who has worked so hard to get her people off this planet would never abandon her mission for me. And I would never expect her to.

Even if we could tolerate each other for longer than a few moments at a time.

You tolerated each other last night.

I grind my teeth, attempting to bury the memory of Sarissa draped over my chest. I never thought I enjoyed tough females. I enjoyed females who laughed and flirted and were untouched by trauma. *Light* females.

When you want to harden a piece of wood, you slowly turn it above the flames of a fire—removing the moisture. Eventually, it becomes much, much more difficult to break.

The fire Sarissa has lived through has hardened her, making her strong in a way few people are strong.

But watching that strong female bend for me...the feel of her lying on top of me, nuzzling my chest...

Screams sound, and I jolt, surveying the training arena.

"Move!" Dexar roars, sprinting toward Alexis and throwing her over his shoulder. He runs toward the fence circling the arena, and I jump over it, panic burning through my chest as I search for Sarissa. Relief makes my hands shake. She's herding a group of children further into one corner of the arena, her eyes on the sky.

Dragix lands so hard the ground turns into a crater beneath him.

Silence.

And then the screams sound.

"Dragix! Oh God, Dragix." Charlie runs toward her dragon, and Sarissa is instantly by her side, holding Charlie steady as her knees buckle.

Dragix turns into a man, and Dexar leaps toward him. Within moments, several warriors are lifting the unconscious dragon and carrying him toward the healers' kradi. Charlie is almost inconsolable, and I step up next to her and Sarissa.

"Lean on me," I say, and Charlie does, finding her feet.

"He's not dead," Sarissa says.

Charlie lets out a sob. "He almost is. He can't even speak on our mental pathway."

"You know he heals like a champ. I saw it with my own eyes when he was attacked by the Dokhalls."

"Arix gave him cava berries." Charlie stops and looks at me, and I slowly shake my head.

"Our cava patch was targeted by our enemies. We have just enough hidden away for emergencies, but it will be some time before our source is replenished. I'm sorry."

Charlie nods, another sob escaping her, and guilt stabs into me like a blade. I should have planted more berries when I had the chance. I had thought the chances of the cava patch being targeted were minimal. Had imagined I was giving in to my usual paranoia.

I help Charlie into the kradi, and the crowd clears a path so she can sit by Dragix's side.

"Dragix?" Charlie closes her eyes, and I know she's attempting to speak to him mentally. Beside me, Sarissa sniffs, wiping at a tear.

"They fought so hard through everything to be together," she murmurs. "Now she's pregnant. Sometimes this universe really sucks."

The healers are surrounding Dragix, seeing to the deep wounds that cover his body.

Dragix groans, and the healers' kradi goes silent. Rakiz arrives, moving to his side as the dragon opens his eyes.

"Charlie."

"I'm here," she murmurs. "You're safe."

"Fought to get...to you. And...our...baby."

"Of course you did." Tears are streaming down her face. "He's grown so much since you've been gone. I've popped."

Charlie ignores everyone else in the kradi, taking her

mate's hand and bringing it to her stomach. His eyes meet hers, glazed with pain but burning with joy.

"Always come back to you." He closes his eyes again.

"Dragix," Rakiz says, ignoring Charlie's narrowed eyes. "What happened?"

Dragix forces his eyes open. "Zintas. Their trap was more sophisticated than any I've seen before."

"What were they doing in the north?"

"I took a Zinta after the attack and forced him to tell me what he knew before I healed enough to fly. He's allied with someone called Mazark."

I let out a growl, and Rakiz whips his head, his gaze meeting mine.

"Who's Mazark?"

"A tribe king from Kenritz—a territory close to ours. He's one of Arix's allies. At least he was. However, he has long been eyeing Arix's territory. I'm unsurprised he has chosen to betray Arix this way, although he was likely hoping Arix would be killed after crossing the Colossal Water."

Rakiz's eyes glitter. "And now," he grits out, "we have enemies advancing from both the north and the east while blocking our allies from the south."

The kradi goes silent at that.

CHAPTER THIRTEEN

S arissa

Depression and resentment battle in my chest as I leave the healers' kradi.

A heavy hand falls on my shoulder, and I shake it off.

"I'm busy, Korzyn."

"Busy with what?"

My throat is tight, and I'm barely holding it together. "I need to tell Clara and the other women—"

He growls. "No, you don't. That's not your job."

I head to my kradi. I just need a moment. Just one moment to pull myself together. Without the feel of the commander's gaze on me. "Why do you care?"

He stalks me, practically breathing down my neck as I walk toward my kradi, and I snarl over my shoulder at him.

He glowers back at me, and I throw up my hands.

"You're insane."

"And you like it."

I stumble, stubbing my toe, and curse. "I do not."

Do I?

"Don't fret, vicious female. I know how to distract you." I freeze at that, my mouth hanging open. He almost runs into my back as I suddenly stop but manages to catch himself.

"And just how would you distract me?" I grit out between my teeth.

He sends me a wicked smile, and it's so unexpected that my mouth drops open again. He reaches out his hand and casually pushes my chin back up, closing my mouth.

"I'll allow you to finish what you started this morning."

Arrogant bastard.

"Oh, you'll *allow* me, will you?"

I turn and keep walking, shaking my head at his ego.

"Yes. If you're very good, I'll even let you be on top."

He's trying to make me insane. It's obvious.

"You'll *let* me?"

"Mm-hmm." I glance back at him, but he's scanning our surroundings, likely fighting back his paranoia at having kradis on either side of us.

"Yes. After all, you owe me."

I turn and walk faster. I don't need this particular brand of crazy in my life.

But I can't seem to help myself.

"And how," I say out the side of my mouth, "could I possibly owe you?"

"Many ways. First, you stole the kiss I should have had with the dark-haired female."

Kill him. I'll kill him slowly. I'll make it last days.

I reach my kradi and spin. "For your information, I thought you were that hot guard Heros. You know, the one I was dancing with?"

His expression turns terrible at that, and I take a step

back despite myself. Fury simmers in his eyes, and he stares at me, wrestling it back under control.

"Not only did you ruin my chances with the dark-haired female," he says as if I hadn't spoken, "but you left me in that cave while you put yourself in danger."

"Which part are you more upset about? The leaving-you-alone part, or the going-into-danger part?"

"Why?"

"I'm just curious."

He bares his teeth at me in a feral smile. "You did this not because your life was in immediate peril but because you were desperate to get that chip back here."

"Yes. Because I had a job to do! You know, the whole 'get that spaceship working' plan? I was trusted to get that chip to Alexis, and I couldn't let everyone down."

"I understand loyalty. I know what it's like to put your life on the line for someone else."

"Good, then you get it."

He smiles, and it's such a cold smile that I almost shiver. "No. Because you owe your loyalty to me."

I blink at that. "Why?"

"Because you're mine."

I open my mouth, once again struck dumb by the insane male in front of me, but he doesn't wait for what was sure to be a very well-made point that would shut down all his arguments.

Instead, he pulls me to him, catching my lips with his as he hauls me into my kradi.

I moan into his mouth, and he grins against my lips. I valiantly manage to pull my head back, taking in the way he glowers down at me—his face a combination of fury and lust.

But there's something in his eyes. Something that looks a lot like hope.

"What are we doing?"

"Mating."

I blink at that. "Wait. You want to mate with me? You know I'm getting on that ship, right?"

Strangely, the thought no longer makes me tremble with anticipation at kicking Grivath ass.

He nods, flashing his teeth at me. "You can be my temporary mate."

"Have you gone *temporarily* insane?"

He shrugs. "I never imagined I'd have a mate for life."

"Why not?"

He shrugs again, but it seems more like an attempt to be nonchalant. "That kind of life is not for me."

I frown at that, opening my mouth to explore this some more.

No, Sarissa. He's offering you the chance to get whatever this crazy chemistry thing is out of your system. Take it.

"Okay, then. Show me what you've got."

His smile is pure male challenge. "I believe I already have," he purrs, and I blush at the reminder of the way I was grinding against him this morning.

Was it truly only this morning?

He walks me backward toward the furs on the far side of the kradi. Then he spins me in place, turning me until I'm facing the kradi wall as he gets to work on the laces of my dress.

He deftly unties the laces, pulling at them until my dress is loose and then pushing it off my shoulders.

My dress falls to the floor, and he lets out a low sound that's somewhere between a groan and a growl. I glance over my shoulder at him, but his gaze seems to be glued to my butt.

His hands cup my waist, then one of them slides over my ass, and that same low sound escapes his throat.

Obviously he appreciates all those squats I did on Earth.

I shiver as he pulls me close, his hands sliding up to cup my breasts from behind. His fingers are rough and calloused, and they feel like heaven as he strokes my nipples.

I gasp, and he spins me again. His eyes are liquid silver, and they seem to see all the way into my soul. His mouth slants over mine, and I moan as he gathers me into his arms, laying me back on the furs. I shiver at the feel of the fur caressing my back and his hard body on top of mine.

Korzyn kisses me as if he's a drowning man and I'm his only hope for air. He kisses me like this is his last kiss ever and he wants to remember it for the rest of his life.

I throw everything I have back into our kiss, stroking his tongue with mine as I wrap my arms around his neck. I can feel him, so very hard and thick against me, and I squirm, suddenly desperate to feel him inside me.

He lets out a low laugh, raising his head, and for a moment, I think he's going to leave me frantic for him.

Instead, he kisses me again, his hand sliding down to rub at the most sensitive part of me. I let out a choked sob as need claws up my spine, and his kiss turns gentle as he pushes his fingers inside me, finding the spot that makes me shudder in his arms.

This is really happening.

I'm going to have sex with the commander.

And I can already tell it's going to be world-shattering sex.

Is it a bad idea? Yes. Am I doing it anyway? Also yes.

Korzyn curls his fingers inside me, and I gasp. He laughs, removing them, and I stare as he raises them to his mouth.

"Mmm," he says. "Delicious."

"Dirty, dirty commander."

His smile is devilish, and he drops his head to my breasts, nuzzling at them before taking one nipple in his mouth. He sucks strongly at it, and I go tense as if I've been electrocuted, pleasure engulfing me.

He laughs again as I gasp.

Two can play at this game.

I run my hands through my hair and then gently scrape my nails over the sensitive scales along his shoulders and down his back. He shudders against me, raising his head.

"Inside me," I order, and for once, he doesn't argue.

He takes his time though, driving me out of my mind as he winks at me, pulling back and positioning himself against me. He uses his cock to gather my wetness and then strokes it against my clit, laughing at my gasped curse.

And then finally, finally he slides inside me, filling me up in a way I couldn't have imagined, even though I've checked out his cock every chance I got.

It's more than just the way we fit together though. It's the feeling of coming home. His eyes burn into mine, and I arch against him until he's seated fully within me.

He leans down and takes my mouth, and then he's moving, plunging into me with a desperation I match, lifting my hips and grinding against him. His thrusts turn rough, and he seems to force himself to hold back.

I don't think so.

"Harder," I say, and he growls as I rake my nails down his back.

He gives me what I want, thrusting deep and hard and

grinding against my clit in the most delicious way. I clutch at him, shocked at the pleasure spreading through my body.

"More."

"If you insist."

I thought he was deep before, but he bares his teeth at me in a feral grin before nipping at my bottom lip.

And then he plunges into me, again and again. He twists his hips, hitting my G-spot with every stroke, and liquid pleasure turns my muscles to jelly.

I groan as I shudder, my orgasm turning everything around me into soft golden light.

Everything except his face, and those eyes, still burning into mine as he empties himself inside me.

Sarissa

I wake, choking, confusion making my movements slow. The air is thick with smoke, and I cough, stumbling out of bed. I know enough to get on the floor where the air is clearer, but it takes me a moment to understand what's happening.

Fire.

Oh God.

Claire.

Our parents left us here with Opal, our nanny, and I yell for her, but there's no reply. I press the back of my hand against the door handle, and it's warm. As long as it's not burning hot, I can open it. Right?

I have no choice. I fling it open. I have to get to Claire's room.

The smoke is even thicker here, a dark fog that crawls into my mouth and down my throat, choking my lungs.

"Claire!" I scream, but I hear no reply. All I hear is the crackle of flames as I crawl down the hall, toward her room.

The ceiling groans, and I glance up. The fire is above us. I have to get to Claire and get her out.

A creaking sound makes me jump, and I get to my feet, stumbling faster down the hall and toward my sister.

But the hall is getting longer and longer, and no matter how fast I run, I can't seem to get any closer to her.

I sit up, my face damp with sweat. Beside me, Korzyn is awake, his gaze steady on my face.

Shit.

"What is it?" he asks. His voice is low, careful, and I let out a shaky breath.

"Just a nightmare."

"Do you want to talk about it?"

"No."

I lie back down, and he reaches his arm out, pulling me close. He rubs his lips against mine, exceedingly gentle, and I open my mouth.

Nothing comes out.

Korzyn kisses me again and then runs his hand through my hair, gently untangling it.

"I lost my sister in a house fire," I finally manage to get out. "I was eleven, and she was eight. Our housekeeper fell asleep with a cigarette in her hand, and our nanny had snuck off to be with her boyfriend. My parents were in Cabo after my father had had another affair and my mother had threatened divorce—a big step for her. My father was never home, and my mother was usually drunk.

"They'd added a wing onto the house and hadn't

checked that the new smoke detectors were properly connected. My father had decided the company working on the project was ripping him off, so he'd fired them." I realize Korzyn has no idea what I'm talking about, so I attempt to explain.

He frowns at my description but slowly nods when I tell him how smoke detectors give advance notice of smoke so people can escape a fire.

I let out a wet laugh, my chest aching. "All that money, all that help, and no one cared enough to check if we were safe.

"How did you escape?"

I shrug. "I was running toward Claire's rooms, but the ceiling was engulfed in flames above me. The heat...I can't even describe it. I was trying to get to her when something collapsed on me."

I shift, staring at the kradi wall. "Even now, I have dreams where I find her and lead her to safety. Sometimes, they're nightmares, and I find her body because I was too late. A neighbor dragged me out. I had second-degree burns on my legs, a concussion, and smoke inhalation, but other than that, I was fine. Claire didn't make it."

"And your parents?"

"My mother slapped me across the face. She said I should have taken better care of my sister. She was right."

"You did all you could have, Sarissa. A tiny child of just eleven summers? You were lucky to survive yourself."

"Why? Why was I the lucky one and Claire wasn't?"

"I don't know. I wish I did. But I can tell you your sister would want more for you than a life spent sacrificing what you need for others."

I glance up at him, my eyes wet with tears, and he gently brushes his lips across mine.

I fall silent. My throat aches so much that if I talk any more, I'm pretty sure I'll devolve into full-blown sobs.

When you lose someone—especially when you lose them too early—it never gets easier to wake up, knowing they're no longer in your world. Knowing you'll no longer see them, hear them, touch them. Your pain never lessens— you just learn how to hide it better, walking around with a giant hole in your chest.

"I'm sorry," Korzyn murmurs, his hand stroking my hair. "I can't imagine what it must have been like to lose a sibling so young."

My heart aches for him. At least I was allowed to know my sister. "You never got to visit?"

"My trainer believed I needed to be wholly devoted to Arix. I snuck back to the village once, and my father beat me for dishonoring him. I wanted to see if my mother had had the baby—wanted just a glimpse."

Fury makes my face hot at the thought of how rejected Korzyn must have felt. All he wanted was to see his baby brother or sister. I would've done the same thing.

"I never went back," he says. "My father made it clear if I ever dishonored him in such a way again, he would kill me."

"I'm so sorry."

He shrugs, but when I lift my head to look at his face, his eyes are hard as he stares at the roof of the kradi.

"I once asked my trainer why I was the one picked from our tribe. Why I had to leave my family."

"What did he say?"

"He said I was larger than the other males my age, better with a sword, and easily expendable."

"What?"

He nods. "If I saved Arix's life, my life would be considered well spent. I may have been strong for my age, but my real skill was my speed. They thought I would be ideal as Arix's closest guard—able to step between him and anyone who would attack him. My trainer said my life was worthless unless used to save the king."

"Wow. Sounds like we both had shitty childhoods."

He chuckles at that, stroking my hair some more, and within a few moments, my eyelids are heavy.

Korzyn

I wake with the hellion in my arms, and my body instantly responds, hard and ready. She's curled against me, soft and warm and deceptively innocent.

I almost snort at that.

She opens her eyes, a deep green this morning and blurred with sleep. I can't help but lean down and take her mouth, hardening further at the way she opens for me.

"Mmm," she says against my mouth, and I roll her onto her back. She blinks up at me, seeming to realize where she is, and a blush climbs up her chest to her cheeks.

"I'm in bed with the commander," she mutters, and I laugh, warmth unfurling in my chest.

"Yes, you are."

And I'm going to make her feel so good that she never forgets me.

The thought of her getting onto that ship suddenly stabs into me like a dull knife, twisting into my gut. I push it away and take her mouth again, stroking my tongue against hers until she lets out a needy moan.

She rubs against me, one of her legs wrapping around my hips, but I shake my head, pulling away.

"Not yet."

I throw the furs off, exposing her incredible body to my hungry gaze. Her breasts are round and firm, perfect for my hands, while her flat stomach and curved hips tempt my eyes down...down.

She takes a deep breath, her breasts rising—hard, peaked nipples tempting me—and I give her a look.

She laughs, and her breasts jiggle. I can't help but lower my head to them, nipping and sucking until she's writhing against me. I kiss my way down her stomach, smiling as she sucks in a breath and then lets out a giggle. I raise my gaze to hers, and she clamps her hand over her mouth at the sound, but her eyes are laughing at me.

I lick at the spot near her hip, blowing cool air on the sensitive skin, and she shivers against me.

So I move lower and do it again. And again.

I slide my hands around the back of her thighs and up until I can elevate her, positioning her exactly where and how I want her.

I raise my gaze and find her staring down at me, entranced.

I hold eye contact as I give her a shallow lick against her slit, and her eyes widen. I slide my tongue further down, and she gasps, throwing her head back.

My signal to continue.

Her body tenses, her thighs clenching beneath me already, and I let out a low laugh against her, making her groan. I flick my tongue against her sensitive nub, and her breaths become heavier, faster.

She's so responsive, her body made for me.

I quash that thought and lick her faster as she raises her hips, grinding against me.

"Korzyn..."

My name on her lips is delicious. But not as delicious as the taste of her, so wet and warm beneath me.

I thrust two fingers into her, swirling my tongue around her clit, and she begins to tremble, on the edge.

I frown. Too soon. I could do this for days.

"Korzyn, please."

I sigh but comply, twisting my fingers as I close my lips on her nub, sucking and licking.

She goes perfectly still as her breath catches.

And then she shatters against me, quaking around me, burying her hands in my hair as she moans above me.

Perfection.

I kiss my way up her body, positioning myself against her. She opens for me, but her body is still relaxed, her eyes closed.

I slide one hand down and over her clit, and she opens her eyes with a gasp.

"Now that I have your attention." I thrust inside her, and she's so tight I see stars as she spreads her legs wider. Her breasts are a temptation I can't ignore, and I lean down, nipping and sucking.

She raises one foot and presses it against my leg, spurring me on, and I pull back, thrusting again and again as she cries out beneath me.

I lose all control, almost falling over the edge.

Not without her.

I strum my thumb against her clit, and her breath catches again, the sound music to my ears as she goes tense.

And then she moans, shuddering against me, and I plunge into her, deeper and deeper, until she comes again, pleasure ripping down my spine as I empty myself inside her.

I gasp, suddenly weak as I roll away, careful not to crush

her. The poison may be out of my body, but the effects remain.

"Are you okay?"

"Better than okay."

I have the hellion in my arms, and she sighs against me, closing her eyes. I watch her until my own eyelids become heavy.

The kradi bells ring.

Sarissa groans, her eyes opening to slits. I can't help but laugh. It feels strangely right to have her in my arms after all this time. I freeze at the thought, staring at her, and she frowns up at me.

"What?" I ask.

The kradi bells ring again, and Sarissa mutters a curse under her breath, burying herself beneath the furs.

"Yes?"

"Rakiz requests your presence in his tashiv," a deep voice I don't recognize says, and I sigh.

"I will be there momentarily." I roll away from the temptation of Sarissa's body and reach for my pants.

Sarissa sighs, and my gaze wanders toward where she's stretching, the fur falling from her breasts.

I instantly harden again. "You little witch."

She grins at me, and I stalk toward her, leaning down and burying my hand in her hair as I take her mouth. Why am I not surprised that even this will be a power struggle?

With Sarissa, I will never be bored.

Until she leaves.

That thought allows me to pull away from the hellion, who drops onto her back and sighs.

"I suppose I should go meet Alexis and Kate," she murmurs. "By now, they've probably tried the control chip."

The thought darkens my mood, but I nod. "I will see you

later." She opens her mouth, but I leave the kradi, the cooler air outside helping me collect my thoughts.

Dragix is sitting in Rakiz's tashiv when I arrive, his mate by his side. Charlie has regained some color in her face, but her eyes are still ringed with dark circles.

The dragon himself seems to have recovered, although his body is tense and he holds himself as if still in pain.

Dragix glances up at me, nodding in greeting. "I will go to Arix today," he says.

I tilt my head. "Are you sure you're healthy enough to travel?"

Gold eyes flare, and I sigh.

"I mean no offense. You're our best chance when it comes to organizing our forces."

The dragon nods.

"Ignore him," Charlie advises me. "He's never grumpier than when he's been injured." She snorts. "Except, of course, when I've been injured."

"Understandable," I say. I glance at the doorway as Rakiz enters the room. He takes a seat next to me and slumps into it, looking more tired than I've ever seen him.

Dragix studies him. "I will warn Arix about the Dokhalls lying in wait on our side of the water. If I kill them now, the others will know we are expecting their attack."

Rakiz nods. "It is better to wait until they are marching on our camp."

"I'm going with you." Charlie's expression is defiant, and Dragix's eyes flare in what looks like panic.

He opens his mouth, but Charlie holds up one hand. "I believed you were dead, Dragix. I won't sit here going out of my mind with worry."

He studies her face, and for a moment it's as if only the

two of them exist. She reaches for his hand. "Together," she says.

Just a few days ago, I watched Dragix fall from the sky, his body covered in wounds. From the expression on his face, the thought of taking his female with him is just as agonizing.

The door opens once more, and Dexar walks in. "I've put more guards around the ship," he says. "But we have the one thing the Dokhalls want. They'll never stop coming as long as they think they can use it to leave Agron."

My hands fist at the thought, and Rakiz sends me a sympathetic look.

My hands suddenly itch, and I'm desperate to once again feel Sarissa in my arms. After spending so much time loathing my vicious little female, now all I want is the ability to make time stop so I can spend every second with her.

Perhaps I never truly loathed her after all.

CHAPTER FOURTEEN

S arissa

The sun heats my skin as I lean my head back, enjoying the gentle breeze that teases my hair. After spending the morning working on traps with the Braxians, I'm taking a break with Nevada, musing over the best way to take out the Dokhalls.

I glance at her. "They may outnumber us, but we're smarter. The Braxians know this part of the forest like the backs of their hands. Plus, we know for sure that some of their weapons are no longer working."

"We barely won last time, and that was before they got their shit together and allied with those Zintas. Not to mention the Voildi. There are so many of them now."

I stare at Nevada. I've never heard her sound anything other than confident.

"Are you okay?"

Her lips twist, and Danica lets out a howl from where

she's lying on a blanket on the grass, having something Nevada calls tummy time.

Nevada picks her up, and the baby instantly turns back into her sunny self, giving me a gummy smile.

"You're a master manipulator, kid." Nevada holds Danica in the crook of her arm and hands her a wooden toy to play with before turning back to me. "I'm scared. I can't talk about it because when I admit I'm terrified, Rakiz gets this look on his face like he's about to go on a killing spree. The last thing he needs is for me to fall apart."

"And everyone else relies on you."

"Yeah. Danica changed everything. Having a kid makes your priorities real clear real fast. I won't let anyone hurt her. But I'm terrified we're going to lose this war."

Seeing Nevada so disheartened makes my stomach twist.

"What can I do to help?"

Nevada studies me. "Ellie is going to have her baby anytime now. She's been having contractions for days. The backup plan is to get her to Tecar's camp. But if the shit hits the fan and it looks like the Dokhalls are going to take our camp, I need you to be ready to grab Ellie and Danica and hide them. Get them to one of your contacts—I know you have friends on this side of the water."

"What about Charlie and Dragix?"

"They're our first line of defense against the Dokhalls. They'll be our eyes in the sky. Dragix has agreed that if he can, he'll help evacuate the kids, but if he goes down..."

"Are you sure about this?"

"Yes. You don't need to hang back during the fight to protect the kids or anything like that—we have people to do that, and backup plans for our backup plans. But if shit gets out of control and the Dokhalls pull something we're not expecting..."

I gape at her for a moment, and her gaze is steady on my face. I snap my mouth shut. She's talking about if most of us are dead. If she and Rakiz have fallen in battle. If Charlie and Dragix have gone down. If Terex is nowhere to be found. The thought makes me feel sick. But she's a mom, and she's still holding it all together for the rest of us. If this is what she needs from me...

"Okay."

She nods. "Thank you."

I blow out a long, shaky breath, fighting back the urge to tell Nevada I can't do it. That I can't be responsible for the tiny little life in her arms. I couldn't save Claire. I couldn't—"

"Sarissa."

I blink, and Nevada smiles at me.

"I don't think it'll happen, but if it does, you've got this."

"Okay." I struggle with that and finally push it away. I'll have a panic attack later. "Back to battle plans. What does Rakiz have so far?"

"He agrees we need to be sneaky. Lining up all our troops and marching on each other is a dumb idea. We'll need to make a show of force, of course, but we have to thin their numbers, and quickly."

"We need to start doing that before they get too close to our camp. But we also need to lure them in."

Nevada tilts her head. "What are you thinking?"

"Let me ponder it for a while."

"Hey, guys," a voice says, and I turn my head as Kate and Alexis arrive. My stomach clenches, nerves making my hands shake.

"Spit it out," I order, and Nevada laughs.

Alexis gives me a look, but she doesn't keep me hanging. "The AI system works. The chip has given us back full control of the ship."

I stare at her. Relief, excitement, and something that feels a lot like despair are all warring within me, ripping me apart.

"You're sure?"

Alexis narrows her eyes at me, and I wave my hand.

"Sorry, of course you're sure."

Alexis would never risk our lives if she didn't think we'd make it.

Kate sits down next to me on the grass and smiles down at Danica. "We're aiming for a hub planet called Brexos. The ship has research capabilities and provided us with a bunch of different options. Brexos is full of mercenaries, and weapons from across the galaxy. We're going to need ships, money, and training, and according to the AI system on our ship, Brexos is our best bet."

"How are we going to afford all that?"

"Makayla convinced Dragix to save his scales for us. We'll use some of them in the battle, but apparently, even more developed planets have a need for dragon scales, and we can sell them when we arrive."

"Wow." This just got real.

Nevada tilts her head. "You don't need to go, you know. Seems like you and the commander are finally on the same page."

Clara and Makayla enter the clearing. Clara's eyes widen as soon as she sees us, and she stalks toward us, her brow furrowed. Makayla follows at a more leisurely pace, flashing me a grin from over Clara's shoulder.

"What's the deal?" Clara asks, and Kate reaches up, squeezing her hand.

"We're leaving."

It's like all the tension goes out of Clara's body, and she folds like a puppet that just had its strings cut, slumping to the ground.

Alexis reaches for her, but Clara waves her off, her eyes closed. When she opens them again, they're wet with tears.

"You're sure? Sorry," she says immediately. "Of course you're sure."

Makayla sits down next to us, listening quietly. She's a mystery, this woman. I can never tell quite what she's thinking. Apparently, she designed some of the best security systems on Earth. Agron must have been a surprise after her high-tech world.

Speaking of high-tech... I frown, staring into space. I'm already picturing getting on that ship. What if it gets damaged during the battle and we have to go through all this again?

"I just had an idea," I murmur.

Nevada tilts her head. "What?"

"I think anyone who needs to board the ship should do it during the battle."

She gapes at me. "Excuse me?"

"Their spies are watching us. If we all start traipsing toward the ship before the battle, they're guaranteed to attack. Right now, they want to hit our camp—where it will cause the most destruction. If they see us heading toward the ship, their goal will be to either stop us or take the ship down so we can't use it."

Makayla smiles. "It'll be the last thing they're expecting. Because it'll be dangerous as hell."

"Why not wait until after the battle?" Kate asks.

I shrug. "Because their goal is to take the ship. If they don't get it this time, they'll regroup and strike again. If we take that ship, we'll let the Dokhalls see that it's gone. Sure, some of them will be more dangerous with nothing to lose, but a large portion will flee, realizing they'll be putting their lives on the line for no reason."

Silence.

I sigh. I know I'm right. "Look how motivated we are to get on that ship. We're willing to put everything on the line. It consumes our thoughts. You think they're not just as motivated? As long as they know that ship is here, they're going to throw everything they have at us."

Kate slowly nods. "If the Dokhalls took the ship, we'd be devastated. We'd mourn, and we'd want revenge against anyone who remains. But eventually, most of us would probably start building some kind of lives here."

"That's assuming a hell of a lot," Alexis says. "Since when are the Dokhalls logical?"

I shrug. "We know the ship works. Am I the only one who's scared to leave it sitting there for too long with the Dokhalls marching toward us?"

"You're definitely not the only one," Makayla murmurs. "It feels like we're asking for it to be damaged again."

Nevada studies my face. "Are you sure about this?"

I know she's not talking about the plan. She's talking about the commander.

Temporary mate.

"I'm positive."

"You know what this will mean. Arix and Vivian are going to attack from the west. They're the distraction."

"I know."

"You won't get to say goodbye."

My eyes are burning, and I push my palms against them. I refuse to lose it until I'm alone in my kradi.

"Believe me, I know."

Clara wraps her arm around me. "A true leader sacrifices for her team," she murmurs. "You're right—this is the best chance for us to get everyone loaded onto that ship without drawing attention."

Makayla shoots her a look. "You know, Sarissa never asked to be our leader."

I can't talk about this anymore. I get to my feet, ignoring the look of concern Clara gives me. "I need to go. I've got some things to do."

Nevada raises her eyebrows at me, and I scowl at her. Yes, the commander is one of those things I have to do. Bite me.

But first, I need to talk to Zoey. I find her in the healers' kradi talking to a woman named Harper. She's grinning at Zoey, her dark hair in a long braid, her bright blue eyes lit with fun. I don't know her well, but she seems like the kind of woman you can count on when some serious shit is going down.

Zoey's busy mixing some kind of concoction that smells disgusting, and she gives me a wry smile as I make gagging sounds. "Yeah," she says, "it's gross. It's also one of the best ways to prevent infection we have. And yet some of my deadliest poisons smell like perfume."

"Actually, that's kind of what I came to talk to you about."

"Oh yeah?" She wipes her hands on the apron she's tied around her waist and glances around the kradi. "I need some fresh air. Let's take this outside."

Harper glances down at Zoey's concoction. "Smartest thing you've said all day."

We trail after Zoey, and I can't help but grin at the way she breathes in the air, raising her face to the sun. For someone who spends most of her time inside, Zoey sure seems to appreciate being outdoors.

I get straight down to business. "I know you've been

working on poisons, and I have some thoughts for how we can use them."

She glances at me and raises her eyebrow. "You know, I've been mulling this over for some time. I know for sure I could poison their water source, but it sounds like the Dokhalls are on the move."

Harper tilts her head. "I like where you're going with this."

I smile at them both, pleased we're on the same page. "I think we need to dip our arrows in poison. From what Vivian told me about the poison on the knife you gave her, even the slightest scratch could slow them down significantly."

"That's what I was thinking too," Zoey says.

"Well, I have a few other ideas in mind as well." I tell them both what I'm thinking, and nods.

"I like it."

We smile at each other. "Let's take this fight medieval," I say.

"I can help mix up some of the poisons," Harper offers. "As long as they don't smell as bad as whatever you've got going on in that kradi right now."

Zoey laughs. "They're not all that stinky, I promise." She nibbles on her bottom lip. "I shouldn't be this excited about someone else's pain and suffering."

I shrug at that. As far as I'm concerned, the Dokhalls deserve everything they get.

"I'll talk to Nevada," Zoey says. "I look forward to working with you both."

I grin. "Sounds like this is the start of a beautiful working relationship."

Makayla and Blaire walk past and Harper goes still, the

smile dropping from her face. I nudge her with my elbow. "Something wrong?"

She sighs. "Promise not to say anything?"

Zoey and I both nod.

"Makayla was responsible for creating security systems to lock up some of the prettiest things on Earth. And I was responsible for taking them back out again." She wiggles her fingers. "Without the owner's permission."

My mouth drops open and Harper nods. "Yeah," she mutters. "Oh, and Emma is a cop. It's only a matter of time before we have to have *that* conversation."

Zoey nibbles on her lower lip. "You should probably have that conversation sooner rather than later."

I tense, feeling him before I see him. When I glance over my shoulder, Korzyn is standing outside Rakiz's tashiv, his eyes on me.

He stalks toward me, and Harper laughs. "Wow," she murmurs. Then she lets out a choked cough. "Choking on the sexual tension." She makes a strangled sound, raising her hands to her throat, and I roll my eyes.

"Ha ha."

Zoey grins at me as they both walk back into the healers' kradi. But I barely notice. All my attention is on the way the commander prowls down the row of kradis, his eyes burning as he stares at me.

"Hey," I say stupidly as he draws closer.

His voice is low and teasing, and he ignores my awkwardness. "Hey," he purrs, and despite myself, I blush.

What's going on with me? I *never* blush. At least I never used to. Now, I seem to blush around this man all the damn time.

He takes me by the hand and leads me to the steps of the

tashiv, gesturing for me to sit down. "What's going on?" I ask, and he simply grins at me.

"I'll be right back," he says. "Wait for me right here."

For once, I'm willing to let him boss me around. I have a sudden vision of him putting me on all fours last night and ordering me not to move. Okay, so maybe taking orders can be fun occasionally.

He's waiting for me to answer, so I shrug. "Fine."

There's an odd sort of desperation in his eyes. It's as if he's trying to be lighthearted. And it's easy to understand why. He's just come from meeting with Rakiz, Dexar, and Dragix. And I can guarantee they weren't talking about the weather. My heart aches. If he wants to pretend our world isn't falling apart, who am I to stop him?

I smile at him, and his silver eyes gleam with a hint of relief. I settle in as he turns and strides away, and I take a few moments to watch the people around me going about their day.

I'm going to miss this place.

This planet and these people are barbaric. They take what they want, and they don't apologize for it. But beneath everything they do is their own code, their own values and morals.

Help those weaker than yourself. Fight for what is right. Don't lie, cheat, or steal. Value your mate above all else. Always think about the good of the tribe as a whole.

Here, people argue, they fight—often fiercely. But they love just as fiercely. And they treat each other as a family.

Korzyn doesn't take long, returning with a large sack and a blanket draped over his shoulder. I raise my eyebrow, but he takes my hand—pulling me behind the tashiv and down a short path. Within a few moments, I can hear the sound of a stream. He finds a good spot on the grass and lays down his blanket, gesturing for me to take a seat. My mouth waters as delicious scents waft toward me from the sack.

"Rakiz told me about this place," he says as he sits down, stretching out his long legs in front of him. He reaches into the sack and begins unpacking it, handing me a piece of bread along with the roast meat he knows I like.

"It's beautiful." And it is. There are no sounds other than the bubbling of the stream and the rustle of the wind through the trees.

We talk about everything except the coming battle. It's as if we're both in silent agreement we'll take this one afternoon for ourselves.

It turns out the commander is funny. I've had glimpses of his sarcastic wit, of course, but here, sitting next to me, he seems more relaxed than I've ever seen him. He tells me about growing up in the castle, and while it must have been lonely—especially knowing he had pretty much been disowned by his family—he has me laughing until I'm clutching my stomach with stories about protecting Arix's life. It turns out the king was somewhat of a klutz as a kid.

I tell him about the pranks Vivian and I used to play on each other. "I was bigger, and I was mean," I admit. "But she was sneaky, and she'd always get her revenge when I least expected it."

Korzyn flashes his teeth in a grin. "Tell me about what you did on Earth."

I tense. "Why?"

He's silent, raising his eyebrow, and I sigh. I'm so used to not talking about my work that even now, on an alien planet, it's difficult to start.

"After Claire died, I withdrew even more from my parents. They were never around, and I threw myself into school. The last time I saw them was a few months before I went to college. While I was studying, I created an app that helped predict the likelihood of an area being targeted by terrorists."

Korzyn frowns, and I take a few minutes to explain. He looks amazed, and I realize it must sound fantastical to him.

"I was approached by the CIA when I was twenty. I finished up my degree while working a 'consulting gig,' as far as my family and friends were concerned. In reality, I was reading cables from around the world, detailing new plots. I'd sort them based on their level of urgency. It was difficult, exciting work, and it made me feel like I was making a difference."

Korzyn reaches out his arm and wraps it around my shoulders. "Then what happened?" His voice is low, and I know he doesn't understand most of what I'm telling him. But he seems to know I need to get it out. Need to tell *someone* about the reality of my life on Earth.

"After I'd graduated, I was invited to the Clandestine Service. Finally, I'd be the one out in the field, working to get the information we needed to protect innocent lives. I was sent to the Farm. I learned how to recruit assets, how to use those assets, and how to protect them from getting a bullet in the head—or worse. I learned how to find the best places for meetings, how to spot a tail, and how to lose one. I learned how to flip a car by tapping the exact right spot with my own car. I learned how to navigate through woods and how to identify a roadside bomb. By the time I left, I could shoot almost any weapon and prevent someone from dying from a sucking chest wound."

I lean my head against Korzyn's chest. "Only one person in my life even knew I worked for the CIA."

"Vivian," he guesses, and I nod.

"No one else could ever know, and of course she could

never know what I truly did. I was sent to Thailand for six months, China for three years, and then Pakistan. It was an exciting life, but it was tough. I was lonely a lot of the time. When you're living a false life, you begin to forget who you are."

He's silent for a moment. "This is why you were so good at making connections on this planet."

I nod. "I'm trained to get the information I need. To make people like me."

He bares his teeth in a fierce grin, and I stare up at him as his arm tightens around me. "You never used your skills on me."

I nod. "I didn't see the point. You were already suspicious of us."

His grin widens, and I tilt my head.

"Why are you so happy about that?"

"Because everything that happened between us is in spite of our initial dislike and mistrust of each other. If you had befriended me, had used your skills to make me trust you…"

I swallow around the lump in my throat. "You'd wonder if anything we had was real."

He nods. "But now I know my prickly, vicious female is with me in spite of herself."

I laugh at that. "And that's better?"

"Oh yes."

When the sun begins to go down, we watch the sunset until Korzyn gets to his feet, offering me his hand.

"Will you come stay with me?"

I nod, smiling up at him, but my lips tremble, and he swoops down, pressing his mouth to mine. I drink him in until a cool breeze makes me shiver, and he pulls away, rubbing my arms with his hands to warm them.

Who knew the commander could be so...tender?

No one disturbs us as we walk back to his kradi. The light is dim, and he immediately takes my mouth, his hands going to the laces on the back of my dress.

His hands freeze. And he lowers his head, burying it in my neck. I clutch at his arms, and he shudders, regaining control.

I attempt to swallow around the lump in my throat. My face is wet.

Korzyn lifts his head, kissing the tears off my cheeks.

Neither of us speak, but he makes love to me for the rest of the night.

CHAPTER FIFTEEN

K orzyn

I'm standing in the training arena, barely stifling a yawn. I spent the night losing myself in Sarissa's body. The exhaustion I feel today is more than worth it.

Never could I have imagined feeling for anyone the way I feel for my hellion.

"How are the evacuation plans going?" I ask Rakiz, and he sighs.

"We are fortunate to have such a large camp, but moving so many children and elderly is difficult. This battle will be our last stand. If they make it to the camp, we are done."

People suddenly scatter, throwing down their swords and tools as they move toward the edges of the training arena. I glance up. Dragix is approaching, and he lets out a warning roar before landing in the middle of the arena, Charlie on his back. He immediately raises his huge clawed foot, and she hops onto it so he can place her on the ground.

Gold sparks fly around him as he transforms.

"It is done," he says.

Charlie reaches into her pocket and hands Rakiz and me each a note.

"Arix knew you were poisoned," Charlie says. "He had sent scouts after you only for them to be attacked by the Dokhalls lying in wait. Three of them were killed, but the fourth managed to get a message sent back to him. He's been readying his army ever since, and he'll be marching tomorrow."

I frown. "And the Dokhalls?"

Dragix throws his arm over his female's shoulder. "They will make it here before Arix. They're traveling slowly, unused to moving such large numbers through the forest. Your fire helped with that—they have few places to hide."

"It was Sarissa's fire," I say, and Charlie smiles at me.

I glance behind her to where Sarissa is building something with a group of human females and two of Rakiz's warriors.

"We need the launch angle to be as close to forty-five degrees as possible," Sarissa says, and I frown. What exactly are they working on?

Dragix and Charlie wander away, almost colliding with Dexar, who lets out an aggrieved sigh.

"I see our resident dragon still doesn't believe in pants," he says.

Charlie glances over her shoulder at the qatai and grins, while Dragix chooses to ignore him as they walk away.

"Our traps on the east side are almost finished," Dexar says. "One of the human females—Clara—is requesting two warriors to guard the younger females in case they decide to get on the ship."

Rakiz growls low in his throat. "Request denied. We

need every available warrior to fight. Besides, we would be the ones left with young, furious human females."

I frown. "What are you talking about?"

"Haven't you heard?" Rakiz flicks me a glance. "The females will likely be leaving on the ship during the battle."

I must look stunned because he frowns at me. "It was Sarissa's idea. The Dokhalls don't know we have the chip, so they won't be expecting it. And they'll be under no doubt that the ship is gone."

She didn't tell me. My prickly female is leaving within days, and she hasn't mentioned it.

I mutter something to Rakiz and walk away in a daze, a hollow laugh leaving my throat. I know better than this. I have gone my whole life without making any serious attachments—other than to my king—and it was a vicious, cunning female who brought me to my knees. She weakened me long enough that I almost forgot.

If you let people in, they will abandon you when you need them the most. I learned this lesson young, and somehow it was Sarissa who made me disregard all my rules.

"Korzyn?"

I turn, barely able to look at her as she frowns up at me. "I've been calling you—"

I have to ask. Even though it's idiotic. Even though I know better.

"Are you getting on that ship?"

She blinks at me. "Korzyn."

"Yes or no."

"Y-yes."

I nod, turn, and walk away.

"Korzyn!"

I can't seem to look at her, but I hear her trailing after me, almost at a trot as she attempts to keep up.

"Sarissa?"

"I'm busy, Emma."

"Phoebe just had a panic attack. She's asking for you."

Sarissa lets out a low growl, but her footsteps stop.

As I knew they would.

Sarissa

For some unknown reason, my eyes are hot as I watch the commander walk away. He holds his head high, his shoulders back, and he looks as if he could take on the world.

But the desolation I just glimpsed in his eyes told me a completely different story.

I should've known better. The moment he told me he was sent away as a child, that he never saw his family again, that he didn't form close relationships...

I had so many opportunities to back away. To not hurt him.

Because despite everything, I never wanted to hurt him.

To strangle him, sure. Occasionally, to kill him.

But I never wanted to emotionally wreck him.

Which is what I've just done.

Indignation wrestles with guilt. Of *course* I'm getting on that ship. Why would he think otherwise? Not once have I implied I'd stay here. Some things are too important to give up.

Vengeance is one of those things.

Even if it means losing your one chance at happiness?

I push that little voice aside. And what, exactly, would I do on Agron?

"Sarissa?"

I turn, finding Ellie studying me out of concerned eyes.

"Are you okay?"

"Not really, to be honest."

"Do you want to talk about it?"

"Not right now, but thanks." I force a smile. Next to me, Emma is watching me carefully.

"Nevada asked if you wanted to meet us for lunch," Ellie says, and I nod.

"I'll see you then."

I turn back to Emma as Ellie slowly waddles away.

"What's going on?"

She sighs. "Phoebe is losing it. She's convinced she's going to die. I tried my best but I'm really not all that good with kids."

I snort at the idea that I'm any better, but I Emma to Phoebe's kradi, which is filling up with women. Phoebe has tears rolling down her cheeks, and I sigh.

She's only sixteen.

I shove my way through the crowd and sit next to her, taking her hand. "Do you want to talk about it?"

She throws her arms around me and sobs. I gesture to Emma, and she sends me a look of pure gratitude, high-tailing it toward the exit. Now that I know she's a cop, it seems obvious as she convinces most of the other women to follow her out of the kradi—with nothing more than a jerk of her head. Lace stays put, her long legs clad in leather pants and stretched out in front of her.

It seems Nevada has started a trend.

"I want to get back home, I do."

"Uh-huh."

Phoebe sniffs. "Will Clara really stop us from getting on the ship if we want to go?"

I glance at Lace, who narrows her eyes at me, her jaw jutting out stubbornly.

I wipe a tear off Phoebe's pale face, and she pushes her long black hair away.

"Is that what you want?" I ask.

She shrugs. "I like it here. I don't have a good relationship with my parents on Earth. They sent me to boarding school, and I hated it."

"So why the tears?" I smile as I say it, and her lower lip trembles as she attempts to smile back.

"If I stay here, I'll never see anyone from home again. But what if the Dokhalls get into this camp and kill us?"

"Phoebe, listen to me. Don't make the decision based on this war. Make it based on where you think you could live for the rest of your life."

Lace shifts, some of the stubbornness draining from her face and giving me a glimpse of vulnerability.

Phoebe sighs. "What about the Dokhalls? I'm scared."

I nod. "It's normal to be scared. But I can tell you these guys have so many plans in place to protect you. Even if the Dokhalls somehow managed to take down all those giant barbarians out there and get into this camp, they wouldn't find you."

Phoebe tilts her head. "Really?"

"Yes. Dragix will fly you out, or some of the other Braxians will lead you to safety. We have alliances with other tribes far from here."

Phoebe thinks that over for a moment. Next to me, Lace fidgets.

I glance at her. One thing I've learned about Lace is she doesn't do well with emotions.

"Okay," Phoebe says finally. "I feel a bit better now. I think I want to stay."

"I think that's a great idea. But you can still change your mind right up until the day we leave."

She manages a shaky smile. "I'm sorry, I know you're busy."

"It's okay. Do you want to come and help the others build some traps?"

Phoebe nods, wiping off her face as she gets to her feet before wandering out the door.

I look at Lace, and she looks at me.

"Theoretically, if someone wanted to get on that ship without Clara knowing about it..."

I raise my eyebrow. "Theoretically?"

She narrows her eyes at me. "I live on the streets. I haven't been a kid since the first time my foster dad tried to get into the bathroom while I was taking a shower. I know what I want."

I open my mouth, unsure what to say to that. And then I sigh.

"You're going to need to board the ship before we do. Let me figure it out and get back to you."

She nods, and I make my way to Nevada's tashiv. Rakiz and the warriors are nowhere to be found, but Ellie, Charlie, Alexis, and Ivy are seated, while Nevada stands next to the window, swaying with Danica in her arms.

"Someone's fussy," she murmurs. "There was no sleep to be had around here last night."

"Aaaw," Ivy says, getting to her feet and reaching for the baby. "Let me have a cuddle."

Nevada hands her over and then takes a seat herself. I slump down next to her.

"Charlie has something she'd like to share with the

class," Nevada says, taking a plate and loading it with food from the platter on the table in front of us.

Charlie rolls her eyes, but she looks...haunted.

"What's up?" Alexis asks.

"Dragix and I have been thinking about what you and Kate said. About the planet with the dragons."

I gape at her. "What planet with what dragons?"

"The ship's AI system is rather...helpful," Alexis says. "It has tons of information about this galaxy, including different planets, what those planets are used for, how dangerous they are, and the kinds of aliens that inhabit those planets."

Charlie sighs. "There's a planet called Huldra. It's run by the Lahmu queen—who's allied with the Arcav. Apparently, she's a badass bitch. Her father broke an alliance with the dragons on that planet, so she kicked him off the throne and took it for herself."

I see where this is going. "Dragons."

"Yeah. Dragons."

Ellie winces, stroking her huge bump, but her eyes are on Charlie. "Will you go?"

Charlie sighs. "I don't know. It's hard for Dragix to be the only dragon on this planet. He may be the largest predator on Agron, but he's continually hunted. One day, one of these groups may get lucky and kill him. There's also a good chance our baby will be a dragon. Dragix certainly seems to think so anyway." She smiles. "He'd never say it, but I know he'd love for our kid to be raised with others of their kind. He often talks about learning to fly with the other kids, running through their huge home, and being doted on by friends and family members."

"You have that here," Nevada points out, and Charlie nods.

"That's what makes it so hard. We *do* have that here. But what happens when our baby begins to shift? How do we explain that to the other kids? To reassure their parents our child won't hurt their kids even though he or she may not understand how much stronger they are than their peers?"

We're all silent for a long moment.

Ivy hands Danica back to Nevada and sits down next to Alexis. "So you'd get on that ship with Sarissa and then what?"

Charlie sighs. "That's the problem. I'm obviously pregnant, which complicates things, and then we have my gloriously overprotective male who would be forced to be in a confined space for however long it takes us to get to the hub planet. From there, we'd need to find our own way to Huldra. It's just a thought right now. But this could be our only chance to give our kid a life with others of his or her kind. And I want that for Dragix too."

"And what does Dragix want for you?" Ellie asks gently.

Charlie sniffs, wiping away a tear that trails down her cheek. "He says he's happy wherever I am, and he doesn't need anyone but me and our baby. Oh, and that if anyone ever makes our child feel excluded, they'll learn the error of their ways. I know he'd love to go, but he doesn't want to take me away from you guys. He says that after everything I went through on Earth, I deserve a huge, loving family."

"Well, we're certainly that," Nevada says.

"Yeah." Ivy nods. "And we put the 'fun' in dysfunctional."

We all laugh, and Nevada offers me a plate of food. I shake my head, my stomach tense.

I've pushed it down and pushed it down, but all I can see —all I can think about—is the devastation on Korzyn's face earlier.

The closer we get to leaving, the sicker I feel.

CHAPTER SIXTEEN

S arissa

It's not hard to track down Korzyn. He's sitting on a large rock near the stream we ate next to yesterday.

His eyes are hard, his focus intense as he stares at the water.

"Hey."

He glances over his shoulder at me, but his eyes are still shuttered.

I clear my throat. "I want to apologize."

He gestures for me to approach, and when I'm close enough for him to touch, he pulls me close until I'm standing between his legs.

"You don't need to apologize. I should be the one to apologize to you. Both of us knew this was temporary. The fact it happened at all is still...surprising."

I laugh. "*Surprising* is a good word for it. How *did* we go from hating each other to cuddling after sex anyway?"

He smiles, but it's sad, and we simply stare at each other for a long moment. I raise my hand, resting it on his cheek, and he leans down, brushing my lips with his.

When I first met this man, I never imagined he was capable of tenderness.

Shows what I knew.

Our kiss is slow, gentle, and it brings tears to my eyes.

From the moment I began working for the CIA, I've led three lives. I've been one person to my friends and the few family members I still see, another person to my colleagues, and yet another to my targets. It became difficult to remember who I was.

When I'm with Korzyn, I know exactly who I am.

When he pulls back, his eyes are silver mirrors.

"When you walk onto that spaceship, don't look back. Don't hesitate even once. Because if you do, I won't be able to let you go. I find it's...important to me that you get what you want after you fought so hard for it."

A tear rolls from my eye, and I wipe it away. "I wish we had more time."

Korzyn's voice is very quiet. "So do I."

"Can we..."

He waits for me to get the words out, and I have to clear my throat and then swallow a few times before I can talk without bursting into tears.

"Can we just make the most of the time we have left? Please?"

He studies my face, and to my surprise, he nods. Both of us are very good at keeping others at arm's length—and avoiding the inevitable pain that occurs when you let someone get too close. But some things are worth the pain.

Some *people* are anyway.

Korzyn

I sit on my mishua, watching as the camp comes to life. The Dokhalls are close now and, according to our spies, have organized themselves into one army with their Zinta and Voildi allies—just as we expected.

They're marching toward this camp, hoping Rakiz was serious about giving them the ship. Of course, they'll also be ready to kill as many of us as they can and take the ship for themselves.

Rakiz sits on his mishua next to me, giving his warriors orders. Beside him, Dexar leans against the fence, his face cold as he stares in the direction of the Dokhalls.

On the other side of the training arena, Charlie is handing out dragon scales to the other females. They shove them down the fronts of their dresses and shirts, helping each other position them at their backs.

I meet Sarissa's eyes. The hellion gives me a shaky smile, and I have the sudden urge to lift her onto my mishua and take her away from the danger.

She would likely castrate me if I tried.

The thought makes my lips twitch, and she tilts her head. Her gaze widens as she glances behind me, and I turn to find the blue male who flirted with her walking toward us.

I grind my teeth, and he grins at me before sauntering past me and meeting Sarissa as she runs toward him.

He wraps her in a hug as she laughs.

"Urox! I didn't think you'd received my message."

He smiles at her, reaching out and ruffling her hair. She beams up at him, and I force myself to release the hilt of my sword. Rakiz's eyes meet mine, and he grins at whatever he sees on my face.

"I would have come sooner," Urox says, "but the Dokhalls made it difficult to get messages to my friends." He gestures toward the camp entrance, where a group of Krinir males are waiting, their blue faces fierce, their body language making it clear they're ready for battle.

Rakiz waves his hand toward one of the guards at the camp entrance, and he allows the group to enter.

There must be twenty or more males, and two of them are dragging a large cart filled with pods.

"I know how you love blowing things up," Urox says, making Sarissa laugh, and I let out a low growl.

Rakiz slides off his mishua before stalking over to Urox and his friends. He slaps the other male on the back, and they immediately begin making plans.

Truthfully, we need all the warriors and weapons we can get. But that doesn't mean I'm pleased by this new development.

I slide off my own mishua as Sarissa moves back toward the other females. I catch her wrist in my hand and turn her toward me, ignoring the curious eyes on us.

"Feeling a little growly, commander?"

I clamp my teeth together but nod, and her eyes turn soft.

"Against my better judgment, you're the only one I want, Korzyn. Urox is just a friend."

"I don't like him."

She grins up at me. "Of course you don't. He's your opposite."

I frown, but she raises her hand, sliding it around my neck. She pulls me toward her, and I comply, leaning down.

I know she expects me to plunder her mouth, to dominate, to show every other male here that she is mine.

So I brush my lips softly against hers. Our kiss is slow, gentle, and decadent, and she blinks up at me as I pull away.

"I need to get back to work," she says. "Be careful today, Korzyn."

Never has anyone other than Arix cared if I lived or died.

"You too."

Sarissa

V,

I'm just going to come right out and say it. This sucks. After everything that happened, I never thought I'd be saying goodbye to you in a letter.

But as you and I both know, life isn't fair.

I've been thinking a lot about family recently. What makes a family, why some families are solid with a core of steel, and why others fall apart.

You and I both come from the second category.

But there's something we never understood when we were kids.

You get to choose your family. As adults, you get to say enough is enough and do what's right for you. Both of us have done that—me when I went into the CIA and you when you stopped talking to your mom.

I know it hurt when you found out they hadn't looked for you —in spite of everything, they should have cared enough to find out what happened.

But I looked for you. And I'm your family.

You also have a new family. Arix adores you, and you fit into his kingdom in a way you never fit in on Earth. Nevada, Ellie, Alexis, and everyone else—they're your family too.

I'm leaving my family behind.

I couldn't do it if I didn't know, deep down into my bones, that you'll be okay. But I see the way your king looks at you. I see the friendship and trust you have with everyone here. And I know you're going to have a long and happy life. You're going to go on to do great things for Heriast. You'll have children with your overprotective king and love them the way we were never loved. You'll tell them about their kick-ass aunt who went to hunt the Grivath, and whisper funny stories to them late at night when they have nightmares.

Don't forget to tell them about the time you dyed my hair black. I was a bully, and they should learn to always stand up to bullies.

I'm rambling.

This is the most difficult letter I've ever written. Well, maybe the second-most difficult. Because I'm about to write a letter to Korzyn. A letter you'll have to read to him because he can't read English.

Here's a secret: I'm wildly, inescapably in love with him. And it turns out love hurts.

I made promises to those women. I promised we'd get our revenge and that one day, they'd get to see their families again.

Look after my commander. Because he is mine. But I want him to have all the love in the world. He deserves it. Invite him to dinner with you and Arix. He'll be growly, and he won't want to see anyone when I leave. But I wish him all the happiness in the universe. I want him to have what you and Arix have. Even if it's not with me.

See—I told you I was in love with him. Only love could make me hand him over to another woman. Even if the thought makes me want to puke.

It's time to go now. The battle is here, and you're stuck on the wrong side of it. Story of our lives.

I love you. No matter what happens in your life, always remember that.

Rissa.

I fold my note and tuck it into my pocket. It's time.

I walk through the camp, soaking it in. It's quiet. The kids and the elderly have been evacuated, but they're traveling slowly. If the Dokhalls take this camp, I have no doubt they'll continue through it, wiping out every Braxian they come across.

I shiver.

Korzyn is already positioned on the front lines. I'll be meeting him soon but not until we've lured the remaining Dokhalls close enough to camp that they can almost taste victory.

In the meantime, he just has to stay alive.

Nevada is in her tashiv, her face pale, eyes hard as she stares out the window, while bouncing her daughter gently in her arms.

She glances over at me.

"I just keep thinking about all the people who are going to die today. People who would've lived if we'd never landed here. The thought of all the death that's going to come...it kills me. But if I could change the past and never land here, I wouldn't do it. What does that say about me?"

I give her a hip bump and hold out my arms for the baby. Nevada hands over Danica, and she gurgles at me, giving me a wide smile.

"You're precious," I tell her before glancing at her mom.

"It says you value the people in your life, Nevada. It says you know how lucky you are to have an incredible mate and daughter."

The door slams open, and we both whirl, staring at Ellie.

She holds onto the doorframe and lets out a groan.

Nevada's mouth drops open. "Seriously? You're going into labor *now*?"

Ellie lets out another groan, following it with a curse I've never heard her say. She straightens up and takes a deep breath, slowly letting it out.

"You can't throw stones." She points at Danica. "Cave baby, remember?"

Nevada shrugs. "Good point. Okay. You'll get through this. Where's Terex?"

Ellie waddles over to a chair and sits down, leaning forward as she goes silent for a long moment.

"Tell me that's not another contraction," Nevada says.

"Why?" I ask. "Is that bad?"

"They're close together. We have a plan for if Ellie goes into labor, and it involves evacuating her to Tecar's camp."

I stare at her. "You mean she might not make it?"

Nevada gives me a look that tells me to shut my mouth or she'll shut it for me.

Ellie manages to haul herself out of her seat. "I can make it to Tecar's camp," she says. "But I need Terex. He's checking the traps to the east with Rakiz."

I glance at Nevada, and she nods.

I hand the baby back to her.

And then I run.

CHAPTER SEVENTEEN

K orzyn

The sounds of battle reach my ears long before the Dokhalls get close to the clearing where we will make our stand.

We chose it because it's far enough from camp to prevent the Dokhalls from easily getting to our most vulnerable if they slip past us, yet close enough that the wounded can be carried back to the healers' kradi. The Dokhalls would need to either cross a large river or get through our camp in order to get to the ship in time to stop the human females from leaving.

My gut clenches at the thought. I glance at Terex, and he nods. This trap is finished.

We move back, waiting for the Dokhalls to arrive.

"Terex," a voice hisses, and we both turn. My eyes widen.

"You're not supposed to be here." My heart pounds at the sight of Sarissa so close to danger.

She glowers at me, then turns her attention to Terex. "Ellie is in labor."

He goes pale, and his eyes turn wild as he glances at the Dokhalls and then back in the direction of the camp.

"Go," I advise him, and he nods, turning without another word and sprinting back toward camp.

Sarissa angles her head. "Are you going to be okay?"

Am I going to be okay, knowing that not only is she in danger, but she will be leaving this planet as soon as the time is right?

I can't speak, so I simply nod as the Dokhalls break through the trees.

"Get into position," I order Sarissa, drinking in the sight of her for one last moment. Our eyes meet, and unsaid words linger between us as she blinks back tears, her mouth curling up in a shaky smile. Then she takes a deep breath and runs after Terex.

In the front lines of the advancing army, the Zinta traitors lumber forward, swords in their hands as they walk shoulder to shoulder with Dokhalls. Voildi are scattered throughout the army, but it's impossible to see exactly how many Dokhalls are approaching, with most of their troops still hidden in the forest.

The front lines are aiming for Rakiz's camp, most of the Dokhalls holding their stick weapons in their hands. Across the clearing, Vrex jerks his head at me, and we both retreat further until we're standing next to Dexar's mishua.

I glance across the wide expanse of the clearing, my gaze drawn to the trees behind us, but all is quiet. The human females are hidden within the branches, perfectly positioned, crossbows in their hands. Vrex's face is hard, his eyes burning with wrath. His female is crouched in one of those trees, and the Assassin of Agron has no intention of letting her be harmed in any way.

The Dokhalls go quiet.

One of them steps forward. "We accept your offer to give us the ship."

Rakiz slowly shakes his head. "We changed our mind."

"You have one last chance before we burn your camp to the ground. Surrender and we will let your females and younglings live."

Rakiz laughs from where he's sitting on his mishua, sword in his hand. "As my queen would say...bring it."

The Dokhall waves his hand but stays where he is as his army moves as one, marching toward us, aiming for our front lines.

I grind my teeth. We hoped whoever was leading the Dokhalls would be caught in the first trap, causing chaos as they scrambled to replace him.

But we're not that lucky.

I expected Arix to be here by now. Thought he would attack before the Dokhalls arrived, thinning their numbers for us.

Dread settles deep in my gut, but I push it away. I left Arix with our most loyal guards—a team I trained myself. He knows the Dokhalls are waiting. He'll survive.

But will he survive long enough to join the battle?

Dexar nods at both of us, and our army begins to advance toward the Dokhalls. If the Dokhalls were paying attention, they would notice our warriors are moving much, much slower than their own.

A few seconds later, they see why.

The ground crumples beneath their front lines, giving no warning. Apparently, Charlie used this tactic on a much smaller scale during the last battle, and ever since, Rakiz's warriors have been digging a huge trench for this very purpose.

Howls of pain reach my ears as hundreds of Dokhalls, Voildi, and Zintas are swallowed as the ground beneath them disappears. Savage pleasure fills my chest as the Braxians roar a challenge, and the Dokhalls' army is forced to split in two to avoid the deep trench now gaping wide in front of them.

As planned, our army also splits—Dexar and I moving to the left, while Rakiz and Vrex go to the right.

Behind us and to our left, arrows begin to fly, the tips dipped in poison as the human females aim for the Dokhalls. The Dokhalls scream, enraged and dying, but those that make it through the trees attack with fury.

I swing the sword in my hand and lunge forward to meet them.

***

Sarissa

Terex reaches the tashiv before me, slamming the door open and dropping to his knees next to Ellie.

His face is white as he glances at Nevada. "Can we evacuate?"

Moni walks out of the bathing room. "No," she says, her expression tranquil. "I've drawn you a bath, child," she tells Ellie, who gives her a weak smile before panting through another contraction.

"A bath?"

Moni nods. "It'll help with the pain, and it should help her feel calmer."

"Are you sure we can't evacuate?"

"Positive," Nevada says, and this time, I see a glimpse of terror in her eyes. We both thought we'd be positioned a few hundred yards in front of the camp gates by now, ready for any Dokhalls who broke through the Braxian defenses.

If Nevada's not going to make it, it's even more important that I get where I need to be.

"Okay," I say. I reach into my pocket and hand Nevada the two letters I've written.

"I need you to give these to Vivian. If I don't see you…"

She nods. "Get on that ship. We'll be okay."

I shake my head at that. "If the Dokhalls get close to camp, I'm not leaving. I'll be manning our catapult."

She opens her mouth and closes it with a nod, then reaches out her arms and wraps me in a hug. "Thank you. Go kick some ass."

"You know it."

Ellie is on her feet, moving toward the bathing room between contractions.

I give her a quick hug. "You're going to do great."

Tears roll down her cheeks. "I wish it didn't have to be this way."

"Me too. You've got this, mama."

I hug Moni, and then I'm out the door, sprinting toward the catapult I designed with Zoey and Nevada.

The Dokhalls aren't getting into this camp. They're not getting their hands on the women and babies in that tashiv.

Not as long as I'm still breathing.

I haul ass through the camp until I reach the line of catapults. Beth is here, her face pale, her lips a thin line.

"Nevada?"

"No can do. Ellie is in labor."

Beth's mouth drops open. "Just once, I'd love for someone to go into labor on a boring, quiet afternoon."

"Preach."

We begin loading up our catapult, and I glance around me, finding the other women doing the same—all of us careful not to touch the pods with our hands.

The pods have been dipped in poison and then dried so they'll still explode. When they do, anyone hit by the shrapnel will get a dose of poison.

That means these catapults are our last resort, and they're also the last step in our plan. If the Dokhalls still have the numbers to be a threat, the Braxians will fall back and get the hell out of the way so we can aim our deadly bombs at the approaching army.

Makayla hands me a pod, nodding a greeting. Her green eyes burn bright with determination, and she has a canvas bag slung over one shoulder as she works. Clearly, she's excited to get on the ship.

"Are we ready?" I ask, and Beth nods at me.

"We need to know how far the Dokhalls are."

Nerves flutter in my chest, but I ignore them. "I'll go."

"Are you sure?"

"Yup."

Women begin ducking behind their catapults, getting into position. Blaire gives me a nod, her face cold and determined.

Now all we need is to know how far away the Dokhalls are. Ideally, they wouldn't break through the trees at all, but we need to be prepared if they do.

I sneak back through the trees until the sounds of battle are so close that it feels like it's on top of me. I shuffle up a tree and peer through the leaves.

Dragix soars above me, Charlie on his back. She's covered from head to toe in dragon scales, including a helmet. That helmet led to a glorious fight, which entertained most of the camp a few days ago. Charlie said it would mess with her field of vision. Dragix said she wasn't flying with him unless she wore it.

Unsurprisingly, the dragon won.

They're flying toward the Dokhalls still marching in the back. The plan is for Dragix to thin their army as much as they can so that when the Dokhalls, Zintas, and Voildi in the front go down, there won't be as many fresh fighters ready to replace them.

On the right, arrows fly, most of them hitting their targets. Simple scrapes with the poisonous arrows have the Dokhalls dying in a way that even makes *me* wince.

Those who manage to dodge the arrows are faced with enraged Braxian males—most of them on mishua. The Dokhalls swarm, their sheer numbers leveling the playing field as the Braxians fight to keep them from breaking through.

My heart is in my throat as a Braxian warrior roars and falls, immediately crushed by Dokhalls—one of them slitting his throat on the way. Horror rises, but I battle it down, scanning the clearing for Korzyn. He refused to fight on a mishua, stating that he spent his life fighting on his feet and this battle would be no different.

I catch a glimpse of him, fighting next to Dexar, and I can suddenly take a full breath again.

Someone lobs a pod into a chunk of the Dokhalls' army —taking out twenty or so Dokhalls and Zintas. Through the trees, I catch a glimpse of blue. Urox.

From the wide grin on his face, he's having fun.

In spite of the experienced warriors on our front lines, the Dokhalls have numbers we couldn't hope to match. They begin breaking through—a few at first—quickly cut down by the Braxians. But it's only a matter of time before the Braxians are overrun.

We'll need the catapults.

I slide down the tree and pump my arms, sprinting through the forest. I trip on a tree root but throw out a hand and slam it against a tree, barely preventing myself from going down.

Don't brain yourself before the Dokhalls can even get close to you. That would be humiliating.

"They're coming!" I yell as soon as I reach the catapults, which are neatly lined up. I can only hope the Braxians can ignore the urge to sprint after the Dokhalls. If they succumb to a killing rage and forget about our little surprise, we'll be taking them out as well.

I duck behind my catapult next to Makayla, who flicks me a glance as she crouches. These catapults don't have wheels, so we're limited by how much we can aim them. Right now, a tribe king called Khax and his barbarian warriors should be creeping through the forest and settling in behind us, ready to kill any Dokhalls who happen to make it close to us.

My hands begin to sweat, and I take a deep breath, blowing it out slow and steady.

A bush shakes in front of us, and Beth holds up her hand.

"Ready," she says, her voice low as the first Dokhall steps through.

"Hold," she orders, and Makayla practically vibrates next to me.

"Hold." Beth's voice is firm.

Now I'm the one on edge, clenching my teeth as more Dokhalls run toward us.

There must be fifty Dokhalls heading our way before Beth finally lowers her arm.

"Fire!"

The pods explode, the poison escaping as more Dokhalls crash through the edge of the forest.

Those that aren't hit in the explosion are quickly wiped out by the poison. All it takes is the smallest fragment to touch their skin and they're slumping to the ground.

Where they stay.

Bile rises in my throat as we reload the catapults again and again. I'm shaking as the Dokhalls continue to advance.

If this many of them got past the Braxians...

Could they have killed them all?

Minutes creep by. Blood drenches the grass in front of us. Behind us, Khax is ordering his warriors into place, ready to step in when we run out of pods.

Makayla hands me another one, wrapped in a thick cloth. I gently place it down, careful not to touch the pod itself. She pulls the cloth away, dumping it on the ground with the others to be burned later.

"How many left?" I ask.

"Three."

Shit.

"It's okay," a voice says, and I turn. Nevada is standing behind us, tears in her eyes. "Arix is here."

"What?"

She nods, and it's then I realize more Dokhalls are running this way, but they no longer look determined. They look...terrified.

Makayla loads another pod. "I'm definitely going to have nightmares about this!" she yells over the noise.

"You guys need to go," Nevada says. Two Braxian warriors take over our catapult as others wait behind them, ready for the moment all the other catapults are out of pods and it's their turn to rejoin the battle.

I blink. "Go?"

Nevada jerks her head in the direction of the ship. "Arix brought a huge army with him. Any Dokhalls that aren't dead are fleeing. It's time for you to make your move."

"Where's Korzyn?"

Nevada gives me a look as Makayla begins sprinting between catapults, spreading the word. "He's on his way. You'll get to say goodbye."

"Ellie?"

"She's fine. The baby is fine. It's a beautiful baby boy."

Relief rushes through me. It's over.

CHAPTER EIGHTEEN

S arissa

I stare at the ship. At everything I've wanted since the moment I landed on this planet. It represents hope. Vengeance. Retribution. Home.

"I'm going to miss you so much," Beth says next to me, and I throw an arm around her.

It takes me a moment to swallow around the lump in my throat as I tear my gaze away from the ship.

Most of us are gathered here. Even Ellie sits on an overturned tree, her baby in her arms. Terex sits next to her, the look on his face making it clear he would prefer for her to be in bed.

Nevada stands on the ramp leading to the ship, Rakiz by her side. The tribe king is bloody and bruised, but he clutches Danica in his arms like he'll never let her go.

"It's time," Nevada says. She glances at me. "Arix and his

army are taking care of the remaining Dokhalls. Let's get you guys on this ship."

Vivian.

My chest hurts so much that I feel like I can't breathe. Nevada has my letters for Vivian and Korzyn, but...

Rakiz said Korzyn is okay. He said the last time he saw him, he was fighting on the front lines. If he doesn't make it in time, at least I'll know he survived.

Arix will stay in place—his army cutting down any Dokhalls who still think to attack.

And Vivian...

It doesn't seem real. The fact I'll likely never see her again.

I feel like a zombie as I hug Alexis, Zoey, and Ivy. All of them have tears streaming down their faces, but my face is dry. I feel oddly numb—as if I'm not really here but I'm floating somewhere above my body, looking down as it goes through the motions.

I make my way to Ellie, leaning down and giving her a hug. She lets out a sob, and Terex wraps his arm around her, his face hard. I nod at him, and he nods back as I smile at their tiny son.

"He's beautiful."

Nevada finishes her goodbyes with the other women and stalks toward me. "I'm going to miss the hell out of you."

"Right back atcha." My eyes are wet now, but I hold back the tears.

Charlie and Dragix are next. Charlie is pale as she stares at the ship. They've decided not to come with us—unwilling to risk their baby—but I know she's wondering if she's made the right choice.

"You have family here," I whisper in her ear as I hug her. "Your baby will be so, so loved."

She smiles at me, her eyes sparkling with tears, and Dragix slaps me gently on the shoulder.

Korzyn bursts through the trees, and I let out a strangled sound from somewhere in my throat. He looks like he's been bathing in blood, but we stare at each other, neither of us able to make the first move.

"It's now or never," Nevada murmurs, and I jolt into action.

Korzyn strides toward me, wrapping me in his arms. I manage to hold back the sobs that want to escape from my chest, breathing in the scent of him beneath the blood and dirt.

Our kiss is gentle, tender, and far too short. Nevada tugs on my arm, and I give him one last shaky smile. He nods back at me.

Time to go.

I just need to take the first step. And then the next. After that, my body will be in motion, and it'll be easier to keep walking.

I turn, following Blaire. Her face is wet, and one of Rakiz's warriors curses and stalks away.

I hadn't realized she was seeing anyone.

One step.

Two steps.

I can do this. Just keep moving.

You're making a mistake.

A huge, glorious, unfixable mistake.

A mistake you'll regret every day for the rest of your life.

You'll look back and remember this moment.

You'll wish with everything in you that you could turn back time.

I glance back at Korzyn. He's standing by the others, face blank, shoulders back, head raised. But his eyes...

He nods at me, pretending it's okay. Pretending he understands.

I don't even understand.

I can hear the whoops of the other women as they walk up the metallic silver ramp, the celebrations already beginning.

I've never felt less like celebrating in my life.

Korzyn's eyes are empty...remote. His voice rumbles through my head.

When you walk onto that spaceship, don't look back. Don't hesitate even once. Because if you do, I won't be able to let you go. I find that it's...important to me that you get what you want after you fought so hard for it.

Both of us are secretive, impossible for most people to understand. And yet he's always had the uncanny ability to know what I'm thinking.

And I've always been able to tell what he's feeling.

I stop walking.

Hope flares in his eyes.

You liar. You were willing to let me go—not because you wanted a temporary mate but because it was what I wanted.

I turn, ignoring the gasps that sound. Distantly, I can hear Zoey let out a choked sob, but I only have eyes for the man who makes me feel completely, undeniably out of control.

In all the best ways.

I touch my face, staring at my hand as I realize it's wet.

And then I let out a sob.

I'm suddenly sprinting toward him. His mouth drops open, shock and joy painted across his face.

Get ready for a long life of making that exact expression.

He takes three huge steps toward me, and then I'm pressed against his hard chest, sobbing against his mouth as he kisses me, his arms clamped around me like he'll never let me go.

Because he won't.

It feels like a weight has been lifted off my shoulders. I know I should *want* to get on that ship. It's not too late for me to change my mind. To go with the other women and get the revenge I so desperately want.

"I'll go with you," Korzyn suddenly says, and I blink up at him.

"What?"

"You want to go, we'll go. Both of us. Now."

He gently pushes me aside and takes my hand, and within seconds, I'm trotting next to him toward the ship.

"Wait, wait, wait!"

He glances at me and slows, coming to a stop at whatever he sees on my face.

"I can't let you do this," I say.

He raises his hand to my cheek, his eyes warm. "You want me enough to stay with me."

"I do." I take a deep breath. "I'm in love with you."

His smile is both joyous and uncertain, as if he's been given a beautifully wrapped gift but he's too scared to open it in case it's a trick. "I've been in love with you since the moment I saw you chasing your cousin with a pillow," he says, and I let out a wet laugh. "I don't care where we are, as long as I'm with you."

"I'm staying. *We're* staying. I...thought I was doing the right thing, but if it was the right thing, my intuition wouldn't have been screaming at me like I was an idiot."

This time, his smile is blinding. He wraps me in his arms, and a feeling of such relief envelops me, making my knees shake.

"Sarissa?"

I pull slightly away from Korzyn and brace myself as Clara and Makayla walk toward me.

"I'm happy for you," Clara says, and I blink. "You deserve this. I'm sorry for what I said about being a true leader." She flicks a glance at Makayla, who winks at me. Obviously, Mak has had a stern talk with her.

"It's okay. You guys don't need a leader, you know. Look at everyone here—they all use their unique skills and work together. If you guys can do that, you'll thrive."

Clara's face lightens in relief. "We'll all look after each other, and we'll get in touch if we can."

I reach out and hug her. "Thank you."

She nods, smiles at Korzyn, and walks back to the ship, her head high, her steps sure. She doesn't look back.

Makayla throws her arms around me. "I'm gonna miss you guys."

"Ditto. Be careful, okay?"

She sends me a slow grin, and I laugh. Mak is hell on wheels.

Harper is next. "Not gonna lie, I wish you were coming with us." She cracks her knuckles and sends the other women a suspicious glance. "But you made the right choice. Good luck."

I grin. "You'll do great. Just be honest."

"That's not my best thing, but I'll try."

She turns and follows the other women onto the ship. A humming noise sounds, and the ramp begins to rise. Korzyn glances at me, and I smile at him. "I haven't changed my mind."

At the very back of the ship, a head pokes up, a small, delicate hand waving at me through one of the round windows.

Lace. She got my message and managed to sneak onto

the ship after all. I grin at her, careful not to wave back in case I draw unwanted attention to her. That girl is going to start some shit.

The Grivath don't know what they're in for.

Zoey lets out a strangled gasp, and I glance at her as Korzyn wraps his arms around me from behind.

"Lisa has a flower tucked behind her ear."

"Uh-huh."

Zoey begins trembling, her face pale. "It's toxic. She must have got it from my poison kradi."

I stare at her. "How toxic?"

"Toxic enough that breathing in the pollen can cause erratic behavior, unconsciousness, and...death."

With that flower in a confined space, who knows how many women will be affected?

My stomach clenches at the thought.

Zoey curses and begins sprinting toward the ship, screaming at them to stop.

The other women have already moved back, likely to take their seats. I can't see Kate, but the silver ramp has already been pulled up, white lights appearing beneath the ship. She obviously can't see Zoey, since she's likely focused entirely on getting the ship into the air.

The ground around us shakes as the ship prepares for takeoff. We watch as the ship rises until it's no more than a dot in the sky.

It's too late.

Zoey looks agonized as she walks back toward us.

"They're smart, Zo," I say. "They'll figure it out."

"I hope so," she mumbles. Tagiz wraps his arm around her, and she buries her face in his chest.

We're all silent, as if unsure what to do now. The clearing feels empty with so many of us suddenly gone.

Nevada grins at me from across the clearing. "Glad you stayed."

I grin back. Every step I took was with the overall goal of getting on that ship, and now that it's gone without me, I feel...

Free.

"You chose me," Korzyn says, and his voice is full of wonder. "You're mine now."

"You're mine too."

He's silent for a long moment. "I've never been anyone's before."

"Neither have I. We'll figure this out together."

He pulls me close once more, and I snuggle into his arms.

Looks like I just found my home.

EPILOGUE

S*ix months later*

Sarissa

"How are you feeling?"

Ellie beams at me, her son tucked against her shoulder as she gently pats his back. "Happy, exhausted, sad, scared, content, and in love," she says. "You?"

I smile. "The same."

Nevada watches closely as Danica crawls toward a large rock before using it to heft herself onto her feet. She shakes her little baby butt, dancing to a tune only she can hear, and then glances at us, waiting for us to clap for her.

We applaud, and she rewards us with a grin and baby babble.

We're sitting on an overturned tree in the clearing where the spaceship once sat. Ellie has been keeping track of the days, and today is officially six months since the other women left.

Ivy's leaning against Vrex, her expression thoughtful as

she gazes into the distance, while Zoey sits beside her, strip-
ping leaves from a branch. Since the kids are here, she's
likely working on some kind of medicine.

It's quieter without the other women. There are fewer
people to cook for, fewer arguments, and less laughter. All
we can do is hope they get to their destination.

The wondering is the hardest part. There's no way to
know where they are or if they're even still alive. We're all
hoping they'll find a way to get in contact with us, but there
are no guarantees.

Of course, some of the women stayed. And they've had
culture shock to deal with, along with the knowledge that
the choice they made is one they can't take back.

A few of them have talked about leaving to explore this
planet. They want to see what else Agron has to offer.

Alexis laughs softly at something Dexar says to her,
elbowing him in the ribs. He grins and rubs his chest with a
mock wounded look.

They moved back to their camp a few days after the
other women left, but they visit often.

Alexis says she has the ship's call signal—whatever that
means. But Vivian has put the word out to traders that she's
looking for an old comm screen. If we can get our hands on
one, there's a chance we can get in touch with the ship.

I catch sight of Vivian walking across the clearing with
Beth, and they spot us, switching direction. Viv could barely
look at me for a few days after I nearly got on that ship
without saying goodbye. Finally, I gave her the letter I wrote
for her. After she read it, she thawed a little, saying she
understood but she was still sad.

I get it.

She sits down next to me, and we gaze at the brown
grass—the dirt patch where the ship sat for so long. After a

cold winter, new grass shoots are poking up from the ground. One day, there won't be any sign the ship was ever here.

I can't decide if that thought makes me happy or sad.

Korzyn and I have stayed here for the past six months, spending time with our friends and hunting any Dokhalls that attempted to attack us in retaliation. Now we'll be heading back with Arix and Vivian. Korzyn has had some time to figure out who he is when he's not responsible for Arix's safety.

"Badadadada," Danica announces, and I turn my head, my chest squeezing as I meet Korzyn's eyes. He grins as he and Rakiz walk toward us. Behind them, Charlie and Dragix follow, their newborn baby boy tucked in his daddy's arms.

"Yep, there's dada," Nevada murmurs. She grins at Rakiz as Danica throws up her arms. When he doesn't reach her quick enough, she takes a step.

We all collectively inhale.

"Is she...," Vivian whispers, and I nod.

"Don't spook her."

She takes another step, and Nevada's hands fly to her face. Rakiz freezes in place, his eyes full of pride as he stares at his daughter. Behind them, Charlie grins at me as Dragix hands her their son, his eyes intent on Danica. As Nevada predicted, the baby has Uncle Dragix wrapped around her little finger.

Another step. Danica looks surprised, and then she takes another four steps before falling on her butt.

She grins at her father and claps for herself.

Rakiz picks her up as Nevada gets to her feet, tears in her eyes.

"She walked!"

"She did."

"You're so clever," she coos as Danica claps some more. "My baby is a genius," she announces, and we all laugh.

Charlie plops down on the grass on my other side, dark circles beneath her eyes.

"How are you doing?" I ask.

"Oh, you know, I've always thought sleep was overrated anyway." She grins at me as Dragix positions himself behind her.

"Have you come up with a name yet?" I can't help but grin as everyone goes quiet, waiting for Charlie's answer. This baby has been called Bubba for weeks now while Dragix and Charlie made up their minds.

"Meet Casix," she says. "After Dragix's dad. Cas for short."

"I love it."

Baby Cas opens his eyes as I lean over, and I gasp. They're now a rich, bright gold.

"His eyes have changed already?"

"Yep. Now he looks even more like his daddy. This kid has none of me in him, I swear."

Dragix shifts behind her. "He has your smile."

"He's three weeks old. That was gas."

"He has your gas face, then."

I feel my eyes widen as Charlie bursts out laughing.

Javir saunters up to us, and Danica squeals. She's obsessed with the teenager, much to his dismay.

"Uppy!" she demands, and he rolls his eyes but picks her up, flashing a quick grin at her when she showers his face with kisses. He places her on the ground and sits next to Beth, who reaches out and smooths her hand over his hair.

Danica stares at Cas, and he watches her. She babbles some more and crawls over to us, using my knee to pull herself up to her feet.

"Do you want to say hi to the baby?" I ask her gently, and she leans forward, patting Cas on the head.

"Bubuh."

"Yes, that's—whoa!"

A spark of gold, and Charlie is holding a teeny baby dragon.

Danica lets out a squeal and falls back on her butt, her mouth a surprised *O*.

Charlie's face drains of color, and Dragix places his hand on her shoulder, keeping his voice low.

"Don't panic or you'll scare him. He can't fly yet, but he instinctively knows how to shift. This usually doesn't happen for a few months." He smiles at Rakiz in clear challenge, and I roll my eyes.

"Are they seriously getting competitive about whose baby is cleverer?"

Charlie seems to be recovering from her shock as she smiles down at Cas, stroking her finger down his tiny dragon nose. "Yep. And I'm not at all surprised," she says absently. "Do I need to worry he'll set his crib on fire?"

Dragix grins and scoops up his son. "No. He won't spit fire for years."

Charlie lets out a sigh of relief. "Well, we were wondering if he'd be a dragon. At least now we know."

Dragix is practically vibrating with pride, and I can't help but laugh as he holds up his son, examining every inch of the tiny dragon—from his minuscule wings to his itty-bitty claws. Cas yawns—displaying a mouth that looks weird with no teeth—and then closes his eyes, settling into his father's hand.

A tiny puff of smoke escapes above his head as Cas lets out a snore.

We're all silent.

"This place just gets weirder and weirder," Alexis says, and Charlie removes her gaze from her son long enough to grin at her.

"And you wouldn't have it any other way," she says.

We spend the afternoon talking and reminiscing, sharing stories about the other women. Someone breaks out the noptri, and a few of the warriors organize for some food to be brought over. A fire is built right in front of us, and eventually, when the sun has gone down, the group begins to disband, wandering away to their kradis.

I watch quietly, my mind elsewhere. According to my rough calculations, it will be the anniversary of Claire's death in a few days.

My nightmares have gotten better. I don't know if it's because I'm finally talking about what happened that night, or if it's because I'm surrounded by the scent of my mate each night as I sleep.

Korzyn takes my hand, lifting my wrist to his mouth and kissing the space beneath our mating bands. We had a quiet ceremony a few days after the ship left. Urox stayed to celebrate, and he and Teriez visit every now and then. I think Urox has a crush on Lana—one of the human women who decided to stay.

I glance at Korzyn. "I have something for you," I say.

His silver eyes narrow with interest as he gets up and follows me back to our kradi. I blow out a breath, oddly nervous as we step inside.

I reach into the small wooden box I keep near our furs. "I wrote this for you when I thought I'd never see you again," I say. "Vivian was meant to read it to you after I left. I was going to throw it out, but...I figured you deserve to know what I wanted to say."

He takes the paper and sits on our furs, pulling me next to him. I peer over his shoulder and read the words to him.

Korzyn,

Sometimes, really bad things happen. The kind of bad things you never get over. The kind you can never really think about again because if you do, you'll lose the ability to get up in the morning.

Leaving you is one of those things.

I hated you when I first met you. And I know you hated me too. It's funny, sometimes, the way the universe works. How it can provide you with the perfect person only for you to waste so much time hating them that by the time you're consumed with love for them, there's no time left.

When I first met you, my heart thumped a little harder in my chest. Colors became brighter. Tastes, smells, sounds, everything became...more.

I thought it was loathing when really it was love.

I dragged both of us through the ultimate power struggle because I couldn't admit how I felt.

You're not innocent, of course. You did it too.

That's what made us so perfect for each other.

I came close to asking you to come with me the other day. Came close to asking you to give up everything for me.

But I'd never take you away from Arix. He's your family. You deserve to be happy.

I just want you to know I'm not leaving because you're in any way unworthy. Your parents were wrong to let you be taken as a kid, and I hate them for what they did when you returned. If anyone's unworthy, it's me. You're all that's good in the world—yes, I hear myself, and no, I'm not drunk.

You could've let yourself turn into a cold, unfeeling monster after what your parents did to you. But instead, you let it harden your outside while staying kind and honorable on the inside.

It's just one of the reasons I love you.

And it's why I'm able to let you go. Because when you truly love someone, you want what's best for them. Even if it's not what's best for you. You're going to go on and find a woman who'll fill the void I'm leaving. She won't be as cool as me, but really, who is?

Arix will tell you the name of the noblewoman you were flirting with. Here's a secret: I was staring daggers at both of you that night. I flirted with every guard in sight because I thought it would make me feel better.

It didn't.

But even I can admit the noblewoman seemed nice.

Every now and then, when you bounce Vivian and Arix's babies on your lap, or when you watch the stars each year on Seva, think of me.

'Cause I'll always be thinking of you.

I hope you have an incredible life full of love and laughter.

You deserve it.

Your hellion.

My throat is so tight I can barely finish reading the letter. Korzyn meets my gaze, and his eyes are burning with a combination of sadness, fury, love, and frustration.

"If Vivian had read me this, I would never have allowed you to leave me. I would have gone to the marketplace and waged war until one of the traders took me to you. Wherever you were in the universe, hellion, I would've found my way to you."

My eyes are hot, and I let out a choked sob as I reach up

a hand and stroke it over his jaw. "Tell me again."

He laughs, but the sound is rough. It's a game we play—my grumpy commander and I. I adore hearing him tell me the words he's never said to anyone else. And he pretends he doesn't like saying them, but when he does...

"I love you because you're loyal. Because you make me question everything. Because I crave you. I love you because you're mine. My mate. My everything."

I blink back tears. Neither of us know what it's like to grow up in a healthy, loving family. We're both...wounded. But together, we'll make it work.

He folds away his letter and carefully places it in his own box. Then he reaches for me.

I wrap my arms around his neck, and he leans down, taking my mouth. He's hard against me, and I moan at the feel of his body surrounding mine.

He pushes me back against our furs, following me down. I let out a sigh as he strokes my hair back from my face, handling me as if I'm made of glass.

He pushes up my dress, then pulls it over my head, leaving me in nothing but my underwear.

I gasp as he immediately takes my mouth, his hands stroking over my skin, making me shiver and groan against him. How is it possible that he already knows my body so well? Knows exactly how to make me shudder with pleasure so encompassing it feels as if I'm about to go up in flames?

I twine my fingers in his hair, holding him against me as his lips leave mine. I want to protest the loss of his hot, hungry mouth, but he's already moving down, lashing one of my nipples with his tongue. He gently runs his teeth along it, then soothes the slight sting, sucking it into his mouth.

I begin to sweat, my whole body on fire. My gasps must

spur him on because he turns his attention to my other breast, nipping and sucking until I'm *begging* for more.

"Tell me you'll never leave me," he orders, moving further down my body until he's staring at the wet heat of me.

I blush, but he raises his head until our eyes meet, the expression on his face demanding the only answer I'll ever give.

"I'll never leave you."

His eyes flare in satisfaction, and then he licks me right where I need him. His hands slide beneath my butt, effortlessly lifting me until I'm positioned right where he wants me.

He swirls his tongue over my clit, lashing at me until I'm on the edge of orgasm.

"Korzyn," I gasp, and that seems to encourage him further because he strokes his tongue right over the most sensitive part of me, again and again.

I shudder and writhe in his hands, heat engulfing my body as I groan out my pleasure. He lets out a low growl of his own, moving back up my body as I blink at him. My legs automatically twine around him as he positions himself against me.

He eases himself into me and then thrusts forward, making my eyes roll back into my head. He immediately retreats and thrusts again until he's so deeply inside me that it feels like we'll be joined together for the rest of time.

I scratch at his chest, angling my hips for him, and he thrusts deeper, hitting my clit and making me tighten around him. Within moments, I'm trembling again, and it only takes a few more thrusts before pleasure is ripping into my body, sending me spinning over the edge.

Korzyn's eyes burn into mine as I come, and he thrusts

again and again before following me over with a low growl. I'm panting as he hauls me into his arms, rolling until I'm splayed in my favorite position over his chest.

I never could've imagined this is the way my life would have gone. An abduction, a crash-landing, a war. Choosing love over revenge, choosing to stay with the Braxian who makes my heart thump harder every time I see him.

This may not be the life I thought I wanted, but I can't imagine anything else. Can't imagine never having met the women who understand exactly what it's like to be stolen from your life only to fall in love with someone so different from anything you've ever known.

Korzyn strokes his hand over my hair, and I run my nails over the scales of his shoulders, feeling him shiver against me.

This love isn't soft or easy. It's deep and all-encompassing. It's uniquely ours.

And I'll never take it for granted.

The End

Authors note:

Thank you for reading Conquered by the Alien Warrior. This series has been a wild ride and I've loved every minute of it. While this series is finished (for now) the adventure continues with the spin-off series titled Society of Savages.

The first book is called Wicked, and you can find it available here. While this series is a spin-off of Warriors of Agron, it also includes a few cameos by some of the Arcav. It has been SO much fun to write, and I can't wait for you to read it!

Want to be the first to know about new books, cover reveals, audiobooks and sales? Sign up for my free newsletter here.

I'm also active on Facebook. Come say hi at Hope Hart Author.

ALSO BY HOPE HART

The Arcav Alien Invasion Series

The Arcav King's Mate

The Arcav Commander's Human

The Arcav General's Woman

The Arcav Prince's Captive

A Very Arcav Christmas

The Arcav Captain's Queen

The Arcav Guard's Female

The Warriors of Agron Series

Taken by the Alien Warrior

Claimed by the Alien Warrior

Saved by the Alien Warrior

Seduced by the Alien Warrior

Protected by the Alien Warrior

Captured by the Alien Warrior

Rescued by the Alien Warrior

Enticed by the Alien Warrior

Conquered by the Alien Warrior

The Society of Savages Series

Wicked

Depraved

Brutal

www.ingramcontent.com/pod-product-compliance
Lightning Source LLC
Chambersburg PA
CBHW051224210726

48290CB00003B/779